# SPECIAL MESSAGE TO

D0756268

## THE ULVERSCROFT FO

**(registered UK charity number 264873)**
was established in 1972 to provide funds for
research, diagnosis and treatment of eye diseases.
Examples of major projects funded by
the Ulverscroft Foundation are:-

The Children's Eye Unit at Moorfields Eye
Hospital, London
The Ulverscroft Children's Eye Unit at Great
Ormond Street Hospital for Sick Children
Funding research into eye diseases and
treatment at the Department of Ophthalmology,
University of Leicester
The Ulverscroft Vision Research Group,
Institute of Child Health
Twin operating theatres at the Western
Ophthalmic Hospital, London
The Chair of Ophthalmology at the Royal
Australian College of Ophthalmologists

ou can help further the work of the Foundation
by making a donation or leaving a legacy.
very contribution is gratefully received. If you
vould like to help support the Foundation or
require further information, please contact:

## THE ULVERSCROFT FOUNDATION
**The Green, Bradgate Road, Anstey**
**Leicester LE7 7FU, England**
**Tel: (0116) 236 4325**

website ̴ ̴ ̴ ̴ ̴ ̴ ̴oft.com

C161027850

Born in Warwickshire, Heather Graves has spent a great part of her adult life in Australia, where she lives with her husband and daughter. The daughter of a man who maintained a lifelong interest in horse-racing, she now regularly attends races in Melbourne.

# RIDING THE STORM

The Lanigan brothers are consumed by a fierce rivalry: both love the same woman, and both covet the same beautiful race-horse, Hunter's Moon. When Robert is the loser for the second time, he exacts a terrible revenge upon Peter — engineering his death, and acquiring Hunter's Moon for himself . . . Months later, still mourning his father, Peter's son Ryan is orphaned by a cyclone which rages through Queensland, killing his mother and destroying his home and livelihood. Val, Robert's kindly wife, offers him sanctuary in her home in Melbourne. Whilst Ryan detests the idea of living with his uncle, it's his only chance to see his beloved Hunter's Moon again . . .

HEATHER GRAVES

# RIDING THE STORM

*Complete and Unabridged*

# ULVERSCROFT
*Leicester*

First published in Great Britain in 2015 by
Robert Hale Limited
London

First Large Print Edition
published 2016
by arrangement with
Robert Hale Limited
London

A catalogue record for this book is available
from the British Library.

ISBN 978–1–4448–2940–2

Published by
F. A. Thorpe (Publishing)
Anstey, Leicestershire

Set by Words & Graphics Ltd.
Anstey, Leicestershire
Printed and bound in Great Britain by
T. J. International Ltd., Padstow, Cornwall

This book is printed on acid-free paper

# Prologue

'This is great,' Ryan sighed contentedly, looking at the clear, turquoise waters slapping the hull as his friend steered the motor launch towards their favourite offshore fishing ground. 'All we need is for the fish to be biting today.'

Mike pulled a wry face. 'Time was when putting a boat in the water meant the certainty of catching a fish. But between the crown-of-thorns starfish and the coal mining, very soon there won't be much left alive on the Barrier Reef. Some of the islands already have nothing but dead coral — '

Ryan cursed himself for setting Mike off on his favourite hobbyhorse. A fierce conservationist and keen amateur fisherman, he despised the politicians who were selling out to big business and allowing dredging and coal mining far too close to the reef they had grown up on.

'This is one of the remaining wonders of the world,' Mike went on. 'Those stupid old men in Canberra don't care. They're still in denial about global warming, but it's obvious that the ice caps are melting and some of the snow grounds in the northern hemisphere are green again. Tourists have been going to see it.'

'You're preaching to the converted, mate.' Ryan's sympathies were with Mike but he'd heard these arguments too many times before. 'Maybe you can make a difference when you're a world-famous surgeon. Perhaps people will listen to you then.'

'That's still a long way off,' Mike sighed. 'I've only just completed my bachelor degree. Sometimes I wish I didn't care about this place so much. If only I could be more laid back about it, like you.'

Ryan shook his head. 'I do care, I just don't believe in stressing about things that I can't affect.'

'Because you live here all the time. You don't notice the subtle differences in the shoreline but I saw it straight away.' Mike was back home in Canesville to visit his father after spending a gap year travelling, before heading back to Melbourne to study medicine. They had known one another since primary school although Ryan's family lived more simply, unable to afford such luxuries as this elegant boat; a rich man's toy, built for speed.

They were close as brothers although Mike had been sent away to boarding school when his parents split up. They had always supported each other, falling into the same easy friendship whenever Mike came home.

At twenty years of age, both lads were the picture of muscular good health but the brooding, dark-haired Mike was always first choice with the girls, who seemed to find Ryan's open-faced, sandy-haired looks less appealing. Ryan didn't care; he was amused by his friend's almost legendary success with the opposite sex and his own heart had never been touched, let alone broken.

'Anyway, how's that girl you were seeing in Brisbane?' Ryan asked. 'I've forgotten her name — '

Momentarily, his friend's smile faltered and he looked less than comfortable as he cut the engine and gave his attention to dropping anchor in a safe spot. Avoiding Ryan's gaze, he set about baiting some hooks. 'It didn't work out. I just wanted to have a bit of fun — but you know women.'

'Not the way you do. What happened this time?'

'When I told her I was heading back down south to study, she wanted to come too, said we should get a flat together. Like I said, I just wanted to have some fun, it's too soon for me to start setting up house with someone.'

'Thinking about all those new hotties you're going to meet in Melbourne?'

'Well, I may have wanted to keep my options open.' Mike smiled cheekily. 'I told her I'd be back to see her during the holidays.'

'And that wasn't enough for her, I suppose?'

He shook his head. 'Next thing I know she's making up some story about being pregnant.'

'But she wasn't, right?'

Mike shrugged. 'Probably not, we were always careful. Who knows? I'm done with her now anyway.'

'That's a bit harsh, even by your standards. I thought you were crazy about her.'

'Yeah, turns out she was the crazy one. The girlfriend from hell.'

'And that's not the first time I've heard that from you.'

'Well, at least I've had some girlfriends,' Mike snapped defensively. 'Unlike you. But I suppose it's not easy with Mum and Dad hanging over your shoulders at home all the time.'

'No, it's not easy. I've been pretty busy working around the stables, and I don't get to meet many new people.'

'Yeah, I know. I feel sorry for you stuck out there in the bush, poor kid.' Mike gave him a playful slap on the shoulder. 'So, how are your parents doing?'

'Actually, they're at each other's throats at the moment.'

'That's not like them. Who's having the midlife crisis?'

'I dunno. Dad, I suppose. He took Silver Sprite down to Sydney for a listed race to try and get her a bit of black type. Money was tight as usual so Mum didn't want him to go — said Sprite was a country horse who couldn't compete against city-class runners. Long story short, his hunch paid off and Sprite won the race at long odds. It was decent prize money and Dad cleaned up in the bookies' ring too.'

'Great. So what does she have to complain about now?'

'Because Dad went to the bloodstock sales and blew the lot on one new horse. Mum wanted to install a new kitchen and get someone to fix the roof but Dad doesn't care about things like that.'

'Life would be easier if he'd share the ownership of his horses,' Mike said. 'I'd take a slice of the action.'

'Dad's not interested in selling shares, he wants that horse all to himself. Uncle Robert came up to Sydney from Melbourne for the sole purpose of buying that colt — a big grey with good bloodlines — I think he's related to a horse Robert used to train. Anyway, you know my father and his brother have never got on. They've never been able to work together and Robert just loves to beat him on the track, even though he's always got five times as many horses in work. So, when Dad won all that money he couldn't help himself. He just had to outbid his brother and buy that colt. Even got it cheaper than expected in the end.'

'Good on him.'

'He might have had enough money left to make a start on the roof but he spent the rest on renovating the old stables and building a new one as well. He says a good horse needs a decent space to live in.'

'Insult to injury, eh? Putting the needs of the horses ahead of his wife.'

'Well, that's how Mum sees it, of course. But wait until you see Tommy — anyone would be proud to own him. He's beautifully bred — tall and strong, shoulders like a carthorse.'

'Tommy? Is that what you call him?'

'Only at home. His registered name is Hunter's Moon. Dad says if this one lives up to his expectations, we could have a champion on our hands. If he's right, then Mum can have the whole house done up and go on a cruise as well if that's what she wants.

But all she can see is the money already spent. I'm trying to keep the peace but they've scarcely spoken a word to each other all week. Mum's completely lost her sense of humour and finds fault with everything. Not like herself at all.'

Mike nodded in sympathy. 'That's what happened to mine before they gave up and decided on a divorce.'

'Oh, I'm sure it won't come to that.' Ryan's eyes widened in shock. The love that existed between his parents had always been part of his own security. Until recently, anyway.

Mike shrugged, shaking his head. 'These things blow up quickly. I should know. Look at my old man. After Mum left, he lived in happy bachelorhood for years — or so I was stupid enough to think. But now he goes to the gym every day and he's talking about getting married again.'

'To someone half his age, I suppose?'

'No, worse than that. Fiona used to be Mum's best friend. He says he met her again only recently but you have to wonder how long it's been going on. Dirty old bugger.'

'He's done alright for himself though, like this boat,' Ryan said, admiring the gleaming chrome and white luxury that surrounded them. 'I'm surprised he let us take it out today.'

'This boat isn't his. He's just brokering it as a favour for some friend of his down the coast. Wants me to deliver it to someone in the Whitsundays. Can't do it himself as Fiona expects him to go to some charity dinner in Cairns.' He brightened, suddenly struck by a thought. 'Hey, why don't you come with me? We'll only be away a couple of days. Catch a plane back to Cairns — Dad'll pay.'

'Sounds good, but it depends when you have to go. Tommy has a few trials lined up and we've entered him for a race at Eagle Farm.'

'We can work around it, I'm sure. Go on, it'll be fun. We'll have a big night out afterwards, get horribly drunk and meet a few girls. Come on, I'll show you how the other half lives.'

Ryan's line gave a sudden jerk, catching his attention. 'Whoa — hold that thought, I've got a bite. Feels like a big one, can you pass me some gloves?'

Mike tossed him a pair and Ryan settled in for a long battle, playing his fish and gradually drawing it closer and closer to the boat. This was the excitement they'd come for. They saw occasional flashes of luminous pink scales as the fish drew closer to the boat until all of a sudden, the frantic activity stopped and the line went slack.

'Damn.' He swore softly. 'It's gone. Didn't even get to see what it was.'

'Not your fault, bro. There's the culprit. Look.' Mike pointed to a dark shape in the water, cruising a few yards behind them. 'Tiger shark. Might as well up anchor and find ourselves another spot. If we stay, he'll just hang around waiting for us to catch another for him.'

Ryan searched the horizon, noting a fresh, cool breeze coming in from the east. 'We might not want to be out here much longer, the weather's going to change soon.'

Mike followed his gaze and spotted the same dark clouds. 'Should be OK, it's just a bit of rain. Give it another hour or so, then we'll head back.' So saying, he pressed various buttons to bring the anchor up, started the engine with a satisfying roar and they set off again at speed, hoping to leave the shark and the storm behind them.

# 1

Chrissie arose to a beautiful sunny morning, cooled by a soft southern breeze. Summer in Melbourne could often be hot and oppressive, forcing people to live behind closed curtains and blinds, praying for the hot winds from the north to abate and the stifling heatwave to come to an end. But this was a perfect day for the shopping expedition she had been planning for weeks, timed to coincide with her father's absence in Sydney. As well as racing a mare, he had gone to check out a promising colt he was hoping to buy and wasn't expected home for several days.

For his wife and daughter, life at home was less tense without his critical, often unnerving presence. When they were done with their shopping, Chrissie thought they might stay in town to see a movie or perhaps have dinner at a pub on the way home. A pair of confirmed shopaholics, they were known for encouraging each other's impulse to buy.

'It's only money.' Val would laugh recklessly. 'Plenty more where that came from.' But all too often it would end in tears when

Robert caught sight of her bills. It suited him to forget that he owed much of the prosperity of his stables to the large sum of money Val had inherited from her father.

But this morning their expedition was justifiable and guilt free. Chrissie needed shoes and accessories for her wedding, due to take place in less than six weeks. She wanted Valerie, as the bride's mother, to shine for once and wear something stunning. Her mother's taste in clothing leaned towards the conservative, favouring neutral colours like navy and beige — as a rule she tried not to stand out from the crowd. But Chrissie intended her to wear something other than the dowdy little suits she wore to the races. And afterwards, if they had any energy left, she wanted to choose something glamorous to wear on her honeymoon in Paris. Paris! Her heart lifted at the thought of it.

The honeymoon in Paris had been Tony's idea and she loved him for it, in spite of the fact that she would be paying for most of it herself. As he reminded her constantly, as a newly qualified lawyer, she earned far more than he did, so wasn't it only fair that she should pick up their bills? All the same, this was a closely kept secret. She didn't want her parents — her father particularly — to find out she would be paying for their visit to

France. She could hear him now, making sarcastic remarks and saying Tony was marrying her because she was an easy meal ticket. She didn't like to think that it might be true.

To gain the most amount of time at the shopping centre, they would have to leave home early. The fashionable boutiques they craved were a long way from the outskirts of Melbourne where they lived. The thought of a whole day to shop at their leisure stretched before them invitingly and they were fortifying themselves with a light breakfast of coffee and toast before leaving. Instead of the casual clothes they usually wore at home and around the stables, they were fully made up and dressed in their black city suits, complete with stockings and high heels. Tempting as it might be to face a long day at the shops wearing trainers, T-shirts and jeans, experience had taught them that shop assistants judged their customers by the cut of their clothes. They'd receive better attention if they looked businesslike and well dressed.

Just as they were about to leave, they heard someone burst into the house through the back door, slamming it hard enough to make the windows rattle. Chrissie looked up, meeting her mother's startled gaze. It could only be her father. No one else would treat their home with so little respect. Damn, she swore silently. Trust him to come home two days early and in a foul mood. She watched her mother's expression fade and all the pleasure and anticipation drain out of her as she sighed and slumped in her seat. Home early, Robert would take over, filling the room with his presence, demanding a meal and expecting Val to put her own plans on hold to attend to his needs.

They already knew the horse he had taken to Sydney with such high hopes had failed miserably in a listed race that she had been favoured to win. Now the disappointed owners wanted to sell her rather than pay the expense of transporting her back to Melbourne, leaving him with one less horse to train. But even that setback wasn't enough to account for his evil mood.

Chrissie recovered more quickly than her mother when Robert came into the room.

'Hi, Dad!' she said, sounding a lot more enthusiastic than she felt. 'You're home early. That's great.'

'Is it?' he said, not offering a greeting to either of them. 'And where are you off to, all dressed up while my back is turned? I hope you're not thinking of shopping again, Val, with that maxed-out credit card?'

Valerie blushed and flinched. It was

Chrissie who came to stand between them, answering him.

'And hello to you too, Dad. No good asking if you had a pleasant trip. Just don't take it out on Mum. If things didn't go so well for you in Sydney, it isn't her fault.'

Robert scowled but she went on before he could speak. 'And in case you've forgotten, I'm getting married to Tony in less than two months. I want Mum to have something decent to wear that's not over ten years old.'

Robert grunted. 'Waste of money, I call it — all that fuss for one day.'

'You don't have to call it anything because I'm paying.'

Robert's expression cleared. 'You mean it? For the whole day?'

'No, Dad, of course not.' Chrissie felt suddenly weary of his stingy attitude. 'Just for the clothes.'

He nodded and sat at the table, leaning back and addressing his wife. 'Rustle us up some bacon an' eggs, luv. I'm starved.'

Obediently, Valerie stood up and went to open the fridge.

'Leave it, Mum,' Chrissie said, taking charge and reminding herself that she was, after all, a professional in her own right and capable of standing up for herself and her mother as well, if need be. 'If Dad's hungry,

I'm sure he can make breakfast for himself. He's probably already had one on the plane. I can't put this off any longer. I'm going shopping for my wedding and I don't want to do it alone. I need your opinion and you're coming with me as we planned.' She folded her arms and looked from one parent to the other, hoping her mother wouldn't back down.

Valerie bit her lip. 'Oh, Chrissie, now your dad's home I'm not so sure. Maybe this time you should go on your own.'

'Leaving you here with him in this mood? I don't think so.'

'What are you implying?' Robert's face reddened with rage. 'I've never raised a hand to your mother and don't you dare suggest it.'

'Not that you haven't come close.' Once more Chrissie squared up to him. 'Children aren't deaf, you know. As a kid, I used to lie under the covers and cringe when I heard you raging at her when you were drunk.'

'I can hold my liquor — I never get drunk.'

'Haven't been caught yet, you mean. I've seen you driving under the influence more than once.'

Robert sat back and smiled. It wasn't pleasant but Chrissie held his gaze. 'I hope young Tony knows what he's let himself in for. You're turning into a proper bully, my girl.'

'Yeah, well. I've had a good teacher, haven't

I?' This was Chrissie's parting shot as she headed for the door. 'Come along, Mum.'

'But don't you want to know why I'm home early?' Robert was grasping at straws now, sounding almost plaintive.

'I'm sure it'll keep till tonight.' Chrissie thrust her mother's handbag into her hands and gave her a push towards the door. 'Just hold the thought until then.'

⋆　⋆　⋆

As they drove towards town, Valerie had little to say, remaining lost in her thoughts. Chrissie couldn't help thinking how different it would have been if they'd been able to get away before Robert came home. Her mother would have been chattering happily, looking forward to window-shopping as much as anything else. It was a long time since she'd seen anything resembling luxury or visited a boutique. Chrissie had been looking forward to giving her mother this treat and was silently cursing her father for ruining it.

She and Valerie were two of a kind, not exactly beautiful but also far from plain. The Welsh heritage they shared had given them small breasts and plump thighs. Chrissie had soft, brown curls, framing even features and a small but determined chin. Her greatest asset was a pair of soulful, dark-brown eyes, fringed with long lashes. It annoyed her when people assumed they were false. She tried to remember to smile, as she had been told often that she could look quite fierce and forbidding when her face was in repose. People were always making a joke of it, saying, 'Cheer up — it might never happen' and children in shopping centres would burst into tears when she glared at them for having tantrums and making a noise. Heads didn't turn when she walked through a crowd and she knew herself to be unremarkable, forgettable even. But by some miracle Tony loved her and in less than two months now they'd be in Paris on their honeymoon. A warning voice at the back of her mind kept telling her it was all too good to be true but she did her best to ignore it.

With a jolt, she realized they had both been lost in their thoughts for some time, almost hypnotized by the motorway and the drone of the cars alongside them.

'You OK, Mum?' she said at last. 'You're awfully quiet.'

'You never said.' Valerie sounded choked. 'You never told me you heard all those arguments — when you were small. I always tried to keep you from hearing those rows.'

Chrissie spoke softly, hardly daring to ask.

'Did he ever lose his temper and hurt you, Mum?'

'No, not really. Sometimes he came close but it was mostly all bluster and noise.'

'Why did you put up with it?'

'Chrissie, it was another era. People saw things differently. And he hasn't really threatened me — not for years now.'

'But he used to?'

'Chrissie, I'm not comfortable talking about this. It's all in the past, anyway.'

'I'm sorry, Mum. I know he's my dad but there's precious little love lost between us. And I hate the way he treats you. Expecting you to shelve all your plans just to wait on him. You know damn well he'd be off to the stables as soon as he'd eaten and you wouldn't see him for the rest of the day. He treats you like an unpaid servant or worse.'

'Maybe. But he has old-fashioned expecta-tions — 'A woman's place is in the home' and all that.'

'It's downright medieval. And in any case, you grew up with horses just as he did and you're far more intuitive. You could be a much better trainer than he is, if you were allowed to be.'

'But that wasn't my choice. I took a back seat when I found I was pregnant with you. Robert isn't to blame for everything.'

'No. Just ninety per cent of it.'

'You don't understand. I wasn't his first choice and I knew it. I've never told you this before, but he wanted to marry Joanne.'

'Uncle Peter's wife? You're kidding me.'

'Oh, no.' Valerie sighed. 'I suppose you can hardly remember her. You wouldn't have been more than an infant when they took off and went to North Queensland. When the brothers fell out for the last time, Pete wanted to put as many miles between them as he could. He said he didn't care if he never saw Robert again.'

'I think I remember Joanne. Or I have an impression of her. A pretty woman with long fair hair who always wore floaty clothes. I thought she looked like a fairy.'

'She was fey all right. Beautiful, artistic and with no practical skills at all. Poor old Pete. She won't have improved with age. People don't, you know. We were all kids of racing people, so we went around in a gang when we were young. Joanne was Robert's girl to begin with but he came on too strong and frightened her off. It was Pete who picked up the pieces and comforted her. The rest you know. Feeling he'd somehow lost face, Rob took it out on Pete, making his life a misery. So Pete sold his share of the stables to him — for next to nothing, of course — and took

Joanne to make a new life up north. It must have been a struggle for them, starting again from scratch. Not that Robert cared. I think he wanted Joanne to suffer for giving him up.'

'But, Mum, if you knew how Dad felt about her, why did you take him on?'

'Oh, I had my reasons at the time and I needed to be married — I was expecting you.'

'Of course you were. Too much to expect Dad to wait until after the wedding.'

'I persuaded myself that I was in love with him, too.' Val giggled at her daughter's incredulous expression. 'Stop it — don't look like that. He was quite something when he was young. Not always this grumpy, red-faced git with receding hair.'

'Oh, Mum.' Chrissie echoed her mother's infectious giggle. 'But he shouldn't have treated you badly even if you were a second choice.'

'Well, I disappointed him, didn't I? You arrived easily enough but I couldn't get pregnant again to give him the son he wanted. The boy he dreamed would succeed him and take over the stables.'

'Why? There's no guarantee a son would fit in with his plans. He might have been a desk jockey — a lawyer, like me.'

'Either way, it just didn't happen. And a year or so later, some busybody told him Joanne had given Peter a son — Ryan

— making him more angry and resentful than ever. He was furious that his younger brother succeeded where he had failed. It was an awful time. He wanted sex every night, trying to get me pregnant; but I was miserable and he was tense, so it never happened. After a while he gave up altogether and blamed me for that as well. And then — after a long, lonely time — ' Valerie hesitated for a moment, unsure whether to go on with her story or not. Finally she sighed. 'I had an affair. And was stupid enough to own up to it when Robert found out.'

Chrissie blinked, rendered speechless for the moment, forcing herself to concentrate on her driving. It was hard to believe that her mother, who never did anything worse than max out her credit card, should fall in love with someone and have an affair.

'Who was it?' she said at last.

'Nobody in our immediate circle, thank God. A visiting trainer from England — here for the Spring Carnival. He kept urging me to leave Robert and go back to England with him. I wanted to, I really did, but I wasn't quite brave enough to leave home and face an uncertain future with him.'

'And you were scared of what Dad might do?'

'That was part of it. But I couldn't risk

losing you. Your father might have taken you just to spite me.'

'I doubt it. He's never had much time for me.'

'So we parted and that was the end of it.'

'Do you still hear from him?'

'Sometimes he sent me a Christmas card to tell me he hadn't forgotten. He'd had an unhappy marriage for years but his wife wouldn't divorce him. When she died unexpectedly, he asked me once again to join him in England.'

'Oh, Mum, why didn't you go?'

'For the same reasons as before. And I wasn't certain he would welcome you — he kept talking of boarding school.'

'I wouldn't have minded. I like the idea of an English boarding school.'

'Hmm. Forget those old-fashioned, starry-eyed school stories. Some of those places are more like institutions where people dump their kids when they can't be bothered to raise them.'

'Oh.'

'In the end he got tired of asking me to leave Robert and married somebody else. You should have heard your father crow about that.'

'Oh, Mum. Why didn't you leave him then?'

'And go where? All the money I inherited from my father is tied up in the stables.

Robert made certain of that. And I was the one who had the affair — I was never allowed to forget it.' She glanced at Chrissie. 'Don't look so stricken — it's OK. Over time we've learned to tolerate each other and rub along well enough.'

'But it's not really a life, is it?' Chrissie thought for a moment. 'Are you sure you'll be all right, Mum? While I'm in Europe with Tony?'

'Yes, of course.' Valerie managed a hesitant smile. 'Robert has better things to do these days than waste time tormenting me.'

★ ★ ★

They reached the shopping centre but, after all these revelations, neither of them could rekindle enthusiasm for the expedition. They looked around half-heartedly but nothing appealed so they decided to postpone the hunt for another day.

'They won't like it at work.' Chrissie's smile was rueful. 'I'll have to ask for another day off. As it is, I'm taking unpaid leave for the trip to Paris.'

'It's for your wedding. I'm sure they'll understand.' Valerie smiled.

Chrissie returned it, wishing she could feel as sure. She hadn't told Val there had been rumours of downsizing the office and, as the newest recruit, she was closest to the door. Her employers didn't need another excuse to be rid of her.

But they did stop for coffee to restore their spirits before returning home.

'Courage, Mum.' Chrissie grinned as she parked her nippy little Honda in the garage next to her father's Range Rover. 'He must be over his bad mood by now, even if his trip to Sydney didn't go according to plan.'

On returning to the house, they found Robert speaking on the landline in the kitchen. Registering their arrival, he hunched away from them, lowering his voice and speaking quickly.

'Thanks, Tom, I appreciate it. Tell the guy to call me the instant he makes contact. I have a job for him and I'll make it well worth his time.' Closing the conversation, he turned to look at them.

'No parcels?' he sneered. 'Thought you were shopping for the big day?'

'Who were you talking to?' Valerie said. 'I didn't know we were hiring again. Thought we had enough staff.'

Robert ignored the query. 'Hope you didn't forget to bring something for dinner. I'm starved.'

'You could afford to live off your tissues for

once, Dad.' Chrissie folded her arms and looked at his burgeoning stomach. 'We'll have you in caftans, soon.'

'Watch your mouth, Chrissie. Good job you're getting married. I'll be happy to see the back of you.'

'No more than I shall be happy to go.'

'I suppose you're all sweetness and light around Tony. Poor old chap. If only he knew. Maybe someone should put him wise.'

'Now stop it, you two,' Valerie broke in. 'I don't want to spend the evening listening to your sniping at each other.'

'Sorry, Mum.' Chrissie grinned. 'I just can't resist winding him up.'

# 2

Not even Joanne could resist Tommy's charm. Somehow the big grey sensed that he needed her acceptance and paid her special attention whenever she came to his stable. Joanne loved the big animals and, because she came from a horse-racing family, she had been taught to ride. But she didn't much care for it, preferring to leave the men in her life to exercise and train the two horses. Unless they had trials at the nearest local track, Peter liked to take the horses down to the beach to ride along the shoreline or swim in the sea. Both Ryan and Peter were up at dawn long before anyone else was awake, taking advantage of a time when the beach was deserted. Fortunately, the coastal waters remained clear and the annual plague of sea wasps had not yet arrived to curb their activities. Wealthier trainers with more land would fence off special training tracks of their own and install walking machines or equine swimming pools to exercise their horses but Peter Lanigan hadn't the money for such luxuries.

With the exception of hospitality and tourism, regular work was scarce in the area with little opportunity for young people but Ryan didn't care. Not that he lacked ambition; he had long dreamed of carving a niche for himself in the racing industry but for now he was content to stay at home, assisting his father with the horses and earning a modest living from his organic market garden and pineapple patch.

He was returning from working his garden one afternoon when he caught sight of someone acting suspiciously outside the new stables. On a casual basis, Peter employed several lads and a girl who helped out from time to time but this wasn't one of them. The man was moving furtively as if he wanted to see without being seen. As soon as he realized he was being watched, he left, pulling his hoodie down further to hide his face, taking off with a distinctive, bouncing stride.

Ryan had the impression that he was moving as fast as he could without appearing to run away. Town wasn't within easy walking distance so he must have a vehicle parked nearby, although he had taken some pains to conceal it in the scrub. Ryan wanted to catch up and find out what he wanted, but the man and his transport seemed to vanish into thin air. Concerned that this visitor might be up to no good, he hurried home to discuss the matter with his father.

Peter was alone in the kitchen having a cup of tea and, to Ryan's relief, his mother was nowhere in sight. Just as well. She had a nervous disposition and he didn't want to alarm her unnecessarily. He allowed Peter to pour him some tea before he spoke.

'Dad, we might need more security at the stables. We have two potential champions now and I've just spotted someone snooping around.'

'A reporter maybe?' His father was slow to think badly of anyone. 'I suppose we must expect it now we have Tommy although I'd prefer visitors to ask before going anywhere near the horses. Did you see if he had a camera?'

'No, but these days people take pictures on their phones. And the guy was wearing a hoodie and hiding his face. Reporters don't do that, do they?'

'I dunno. But don't let it worry you. Probably just some tourist off the beaten track, getting lost.'

'Then why didn't he come up to the house for directions? No, Dad, I have a bad feeling about this and I think it's time we had better security at the stables. CCTV and an alarm perhaps. To alert the police.'

'What police?' Peter sat back and smiled at him. 'The local force is small and already stretched as it is. And they'll soon get tired of coming out here every time your mum's little dog sets it off.'

'I still think we should do something, Dad. Arm ourselves with a shotgun or two at least.'

'Come off it, Ryan. Would you really be prepared to shoot someone because you suspected he was up to no good? And while you were hesitating, trying to make up your mind, a hardened criminal would grab the gun off you and shoot you instead.'

'I never thought of that.'

'Well, think about it now. Violence only encourages violence. Expect the best of people and that's usually what you'll get.'

'OK, Dad. I get your point. But I wish you'd seen the man for yourself. You wouldn't be so quick to dismiss what I'm saying.'

★　★　★

His instructions were very specific. His quarry was to be targeted alone and there were to be no suspicious circumstances surrounding his death. It must seem to be an unfortunate accident with no ongoing investigation and the case quickly closed. The accident was to be staged well away from the man's home and no harm was to come to his wife.

No mention had been made of the boy and that was probably the reason he had made the mistake of allowing the lad to see him. He must be slipping in his old age; it wasn't like him to be so unprofessional or make such a basic mistake. Hadn't he built his reputation on the safe delivery of a quick result with no repercussions? Known in some circles only as 'Mister Reliable', he had sent nine men to the grave already and without the slightest suspicion of foul play. He made his moves quickly and quietly, without making a mess. His target would be dead even before he realized he was in danger, and the killer's conscience troubled him not at all. He reasoned that if someone was willing to pay for a man to die, on some level that man must deserve it. To Harry, it was just business. And a very lucrative one as well, allowing him to holiday in Las Vegas or the Bahamas, masquerading as a wealthy man in between wives. It was amazing how such a reputation endeared him to women.

He smiled, dragging his mind back to the present. There'd be time enough to think of the next holiday when he'd disposed of number ten. He must keep his mind on the job now until it was done. Observation was always the key; to learn his victim's habits and use them to his advantage. Unlike the city where people weren't so inquisitive about strangers, it wouldn't be so easy to disappear into this smaller community where people had grown up together and knew one another at least by sight.

Staying longer also meant he would have to camp out. He couldn't risk booking into a local motel for more than a night or so. If anyone asked, he could say he was birdwatching; it would also explain the binoculars worn constantly around his neck. As an ex-marine, he knew many outdoor survival techniques but that didn't mean he had to enjoy them. He reminded himself to ask for a bonus to cover the discomfort when he made up his final account. Then he applied himself to the task of watching the daily habits of his quarry.

Two days later, he was up at dawn, watching the two men exercising a pair of racehorses on the beach. Fucking hell, he thought, stifling a yawn, do these banana benders never sleep? The elder Lanigan was never alone; his son was always there with him, close as a shadow. The only time they separated was when the younger one took the mare off on a gallop to the far end of the beach and Peter rode the big grey into the sea to swim in the deeper water offshore. Their routine was so boringly predictable that Harry had to stifle another yawn as Peter steered the horse back to the beach and dismounted in the shallows, leading him ashore.

All of a sudden, Harry was wide awake, all boredom forgotten. Something had startled the grey, which jumped aside in panic, tossing his head and striking Peter under the chin. Perhaps a crab or a small ray had wriggled out from under the horse's hooves. Momentarily dazed, Lanigan staggered, shaking his head to clear it.

'Dad! Dad, are you all right?' Already on his way back, the boy saw the incident, coming swiftly to his father's aid and taking charge of both horses while the older man recovered himself.

'Yeah. But we really should think about wearing helmets when we exercise the horses.'

'Too hot.' Ryan wrinkled his nose.

'I know. But remind me to order some when we get home.'

Watching them, Harry had seen enough to give him the germ of an idea. He punched the air with glee. He could see now that this job could be wrapped up a whole lot sooner than he'd thought.

Later that evening, his head still aching from the trauma earlier in the day, Peter found himself exhausted. And he wasn't looking forward to the conversation he needed to have with Ryan. Recently, he had taken Joanne to see Doctor Richards and the doctor had called him back into the room without her, wanting a private word. The news wasn't good and he'd needed time to come to terms with it himself before sharing it with Ryan. He waited until Joanne had gone up to bed, having taken one of her new pills designed to help her sleep through the night.

'Come on, Dad, what's wrong? You haven't been yourself all evening and I don't think it's only because of what happened with Tommy.' His son had gone to the fridge. He took out two beers, cracked the top off both and handed him one. 'Is it money again?'

'I wish. That would be a problem I could do something about. No.' Peter sighed. 'It's your mother.'

'What? I thought she was so much better lately.' He bit his lip, struck by a horrible thought. 'She hasn't got cancer, has she?'

'It's not that.' Peter shook his head. 'You know she's always been fragile. Impractical. Charmingly vague, some people liked to call it.'

'Her artistic temperament, you've always said.'

'Yes. But lately, it's been a lot worse. Doctor Richards thinks it might be a form of early dementia.'

'What rubbish. Doctor Richards is talking

through her hat. Take Mum to see someone else. She's far too young to have that.'

'I know. That's what makes it so tragic. Her body will continue in good health long after her mind has packed up. Eventually, she won't even recognize us.'

'You can't accept it — not just like that.'

'This isn't a new thing. Doctor Richards has been monitoring your mother's progress for years. Some days are better than others but eventually, she's going to need proper care in a nursing home.'

'You can't do that. I won't let you shut Mum away with a lot of barmy old people wetting themselves. She doesn't deserve it.'

'Nobody does, Ryan.'

'There must be some medication. Something to halt the process and stop it from happening.'

'Doctor Richards is exploring all avenues. But she says we must be prepared for the worst.'

Feeling helpless in the face of this news, that night Ryan punched his pillow, unable to sleep, and felt incipient tears stinging the back of his throat. The following morning he awoke in the early hours as he always did, except he was plagued with a pounding headache, his eyes were streaming and he was feeling as if he'd picked up a summer flu.

'Go back to bed, son,' his father said. 'You look awful and you'll be no good to me or to Sprite today. I'll phone Melia and get her to come out instead.' And, before his son could raise any further objections, Peter reached for his phone and called her. She was a pleasant but ordinary girl who helped out at the stables and also rode track work for them. Nothing was too much trouble and she loved the animals, always anxious to please. An early riser like most horsewomen, she didn't seem to mind being called at such an early hour — still the middle of the night to most people.

'Love to help out, Mr Lanigan. Give me ten to get in and out of the shower and I'll be there.'

'Good girl, that,' Peter remarked when he came off the phone. 'Always willing to fit in.'

'Only because she's sweet on you.' Ryan reached for the box of tissues and grabbed a handful before sneezing into them.

'Bed,' his father ordered, ignoring that last remark. 'I'll make breakfast for all of us when I get home.'

★ ★ ★

At the beach, Harry was already hidden behind a rock, waiting for the two men and

36

their horses to arrive. With any luck this job could be wrapped up today and he could head south to claim his reward. With what he had planned, he wouldn't get more than one chance and it would have to look right — the horse must be blamed. He had a few anxious moments as they were later than usual, but eventually he saw the two horses coming through the dunes to the beach. This time there was a girl riding the mare. He waited a while to see if the boy turned up which would mean he'd have to abandon his plans for today: he couldn't keep an eye on three people at the same time. But he saw Peter gesticulate, instructing the girl to ride off up the beach while he himself led the big grey into the sea.

This morning, even the weather was on Harry's side. A wind had got up, muffling sound, and the sea was quite choppy. The girl was an unknown factor in the equation; he could only hope she would keep riding on up the beach and wouldn't look back until she returned.

As the girl disappeared into the distance, Harry ran swiftly towards Peter, who was leading the horse into the sea. Wearing only a pair of Hawaiian-patterned board shorts, he hoped to be taken for a tourist enjoying an early-morning swim.

'G'day, mate.' Peter smiled as Harry approached him. 'You're up bright an' early.'

Those were the last words he said in this life. Before he had time to register any alarm, a fist came at him, delivering a knock-out punch to the jaw. He collapsed without so much as a murmur, and Harry caught him to make sure he was still breathing before holding his head under the water until no more bubbles came to the surface. There must be no suspicious marks or any evidence of an attack. His victim must appear to have been knocked out by the horse and swept off his feet to drown in the sea.

Spooked by this turn of events and the stranger among them, the big grey lurched out of the water and went to stand on the beach, shivering and regarding them. The animal sensed that something was terribly wrong.

While he was making quite sure his victim's lungs were filling with water, Harry turned to look back up the beach to check that the other rider wasn't on her way back. This was the tricky part. He couldn't afford any witnesses. If the girl happened to see what he'd done and he had to dispose of her too, it would cause complications. It was reasonable to believe that one horseman could be knocked out and accidentally drown

— but two? He squinted up the beach where he could just make her out, still riding away although the rocks were coming up fast; she wouldn't be able to travel much further without turning back. When he was satisfied that no life remained in Peter Lanigan's body, he tried to push it out into deeper water but it was no use: the tide was moving in and it kept coming back. The sun had risen properly now, lighting up the whole scene, and Harry needed to get out of there fast. He waded ashore and loped away from the beach, trying not to make too much haste and congratulating himself on a job well done. Riderless and unsure what to do, the big grey stood on the shore watching him leave, the only witness to his latest crime.

Less than half an hour later, leaving the other rider to make the horrifying discovery of Lanigan's body lying face down in the shallows, Harry had packed up his camp, leaving no trace of his presence, and was already on his way south.

★   ★   ★

'I don't know what happened, Mum, but it was an accident. You can't blame Tommy for this.' Feeling close to falling apart himself, Ryan tried to reason with his mother, who was sobbing and shaking with hysteria. 'If you want to blame anyone, blame me. If I'd been there myself, I might have saved him. Melia wasn't strong enough to pull him out of the sea. She turned him over and did the best she could, ringing emergency services right away, then she managed to get hold of both horses.'

'Damn the horses! I never want to see either of them again.' Joanne was seated in a basket chair on the veranda, rocking herself in her grief, almost suffocating the little Italian grey-hound she held in her lap. 'And don't talk to me about Melia. I told her she's not welcome here any more and not to come back.'

'You shouldn't have done that, Mum. I'll need all the help I can get.'

'Not if you get rid of the horses.'

'Well,' Ryan muttered. 'We'll have to see about that.' He had no intention of selling Tommy and Sprite, or managing the stables without Melia's help. His father might no longer be here, but he was determined to continue and enlarge the venture Peter had started, rather than part with their horses.

'What did you say?'

'Nothing. And don't hold Tinka so hard, you're strangling the poor dog.'

'Oh.' Joanne released the little dog, which ran away to hide under the table.

40

'I'm so sorry, Ryan,' Melia said when he finally tracked her down at her sister's place where she was babysitting the children. 'But I can't work where I'm not wanted. Your mother blames me for what happened to Pete — '

'But I don't and I'm the one you'll be working for. You're our track rider too. I'd rather muck out the stables myself and let the lads go.'

'But your mother said there won't be any work as she's selling the horses.'

'Take no notice of Mum. She's half mad with grief, besides being — ' He hesitated, feeling it would be disloyal to mention his mother's illness.

'Being what?'

'Never mind. She was upset and if you stay out of her way, she won't even remember you're there. She's very forgetful these days.'

'Well, OK. I'll help out for the sake of the horses. But if she shouts at me like that again and says awful things, I shall leave and I won't be back.'

'OK. If you come in the early hours of the morning and leave before nine, she won't see you. She takes pills to help her sleep and never gets up before ten.'

'All right.' Melia still sounded doubtful. 'But I'm gone at the first sign of trouble.'

# 3

'I don't get it.' Valerie stared at her husband, surprised by the suggestion he had just made. 'You've shut Peter out of your life for years. Why is it now so important to go to his funeral?'

Robert sighed, his expression pained. 'Because that's what families do, Val. I need closure as well as to pay my respects. I know we had our differences but Peter was still my brother.'

Val heard this with narrowed eyes, still unconvinced. 'But why would you waste time driving all that way instead of going by air? I can't see the round trip taking less than two weeks. And time is money, isn't it? So you always say.'

'Because I'm taking a horsebox, that's why. I want to get hold of Hunter's Moon before that boy panics and sells him.'

'Well, if it troubles you that much — why not fly up? You'll be there that much sooner and you can hire a car and a horsebox on the spot.' Val was teasing — not quite believing he was serious in his intent.

'Don't be stupid. They could give me

anything. A box that hasn't been properly cleaned — full of germs and God knows what tropical diseases. A hire car that breaks down as soon as I'm out on the open road — '

'Oh, I get it. This journey has nothing to do with paying your last respects to your brother. It's always about money and horses with you, isn't it? You can't bear to let even one get away from you. If you wanted this horse so badly, why didn't you outbid Peter at the auction and save yourself time and trouble? It isn't as if you're short of money, is it?'

Robert scowled. 'The trouble with you, Val, is that you try to make everything seem so logical. As it happens, I was short of money that day. The horse that we brought to Sydney had failed and the owners wanted to sell it on the spot. On top of that, they'd given me a hefty deposit to buy them another horse at the sales but of course, having lost faith in me, they wanted their money back. And that left me with a cash-flow problem just at the time I needed more money to buy Hunter's Moon.'

'I see.'

'But fate has delivered the perfect opportunity for me to get him back. D'you think that boy has any idea how to care for a champion, let alone train him? I don't like to see a promising horse go to waste.'

'I still think it's unfeeling. We don't know what their plans are — or if they have any. They'll still be in shock. If you're determined to go, we should fly up together to give Joanne our support. She'll be glad of another woman's company at such a time. You should leave your concerns about horses till later.'

'And then they'll have sold Hunter's Moon to somebody else.' Robert's temper rose along with his voice, making her blink. 'What makes you think Joanne would welcome you, anyway?'

'Why shouldn't she? You were the one who upset her, not me.'

'Well, we don't need to go into that now. And there's no point in discussing it further because I'm going alone. Haven't you enough on your plate with Chrissie's wedding?'

'Yes, but we still need to talk this through — '

Then Valerie stopped and sighed as she realized she was talking to herself. Robert had left the room.

* * *

Halfway through the boring and arduous journey north on roads that seemed to go on forever, he was beginning to wish he'd let Val come with him, after all. At least she could have shared the driving. Faced with travelling up the inland highways to Brisbane and beyond, through cane fields, miles of open countryside and subtropical scrub, he found himself missing her endless chatter about lists of wedding guests and whether more people could be invited if they had a buffet rather than a 'sit down' meal. At one point, he caught himself nodding off and almost drove into a tree at the side of the road. That gave him such a jolt of adrenaline that he was wide awake for the next few hours.

He knew his brother's funeral was being delayed to accommodate him but he realized he needed to take more breaks to drink coffee and stretch his legs. Better to arrive in one piece rather than not at all.

★　★　★

Ryan felt a deep resentment against his uncle for the unnecessary delay. He knew Robert had never cared much for his younger brother, so why did he have to come here now he was gone? It didn't make any sense. Nor was he looking forward to meeting him. Dad had rarely spoken of his older brother but what little he did say wasn't good. Ryan's impression was of a teasing bully, hell-bent on having his own way in all things. And, although it was presently no more than a feeling in the pit of his stomach, he knew that all wasn't quite as it seemed. Robert wouldn't come all this way for nothing — he must have a hidden agenda. As soon as he heard of his brother's death, he'd announced his intention to drive north immediately. Drive? Did he have any idea how far from Melbourne that was? It would take a week to accomplish what a flight would achieve in a single day. Why would he drive all that way just to stay a few days for the funeral? No. There was something else he was missing. Going over their brief conversation, Ryan felt as if he'd been dismissed, treated as if he were no more than ten years old. It felt like a verbal pat on the head. His uncle had told him not to worry as he would take charge of all the arrangements. Ryan couldn't help feeling these arrangements might mean a lot more than Peter's funeral.

His mother agreed with him; she wasn't looking forward to seeing Robert either, particularly as he was coming alone. Her mind kept returning to the rough treatment and near rape she had received at his hands and she shivered. As her husband's only surviving relative it wouldn't be right to deny him the chance to say goodbye. She could only hope that he wouldn't stay long. Ryan was quick to pick up on her mood.

'You don't like Uncle Robert, do you, Mum?'

'I thought I did. A long time ago. But now he scares me.'

'Scares you?' Ryan frowned.

'No, that's not quite what I mean. He intimidates me.'

'Hah! He'd better not try intimidation while I'm around.'

'Now don't go looking for trouble, Ryan. He has an awful temper. Just agree with whatever he says and we'll change it to suit ourselves when he's gone.'

Somehow Ryan had the feeling it wasn't going to be as simple as that.

★　★　★

All his misgivings came rushing back a week later when Robert drove up to the house, pulling a horsebox behind his massive Range Rover, both car and trailer covered in mud and dust from the road.

'What a horrible journey.' Robert greeted his nephew with false heartiness and a wide smile. 'I won't try that again in a hurry.'

'Uncle Robert.' He greeted the man with a tight smile and folded arms. Somehow he didn't feel like shaking hands and he saw

Robert wasn't offering to do so either. Physically, the man was nothing like his father, except he was tall. Robert was almost obese, had a florid, unhealthy complexion, lines of discontent on his face and a hard expression in his eyes. There was little about him to like.

'Well, well. Young Ryan, isn't it? You look just like your mother. I don't see much of your father in you at all.'

If this was intended as a put-down, Ryan didn't react, merely gesturing for his uncle to come inside. He knew he should say 'Nice to see you' or 'Welcome to North Queensland' but somehow the words stuck in his throat and wouldn't be said.

'Joanne,' Robert greeted his sister-in-law, pretending not to notice when she flinched from his kiss on her cheek, causing her little Italian greyhound at her feet to jump up and down, going into a frenzy of barking. 'And lovely as ever.'

This was plainly untrue. Since her husband's death, Joanne had diminished. Always slender, she was now almost skeletal and paler than usual with purple circles beneath her eyes. But even when the little dog had been pacified and Robert invited inside, Ryan didn't feel able to show much enthusiasm.

The atmosphere during supper, seated around the kitchen table, was no better, serving only to accentuate the awkwardness they were all feeling. Joanne had provided a simple meal of roast chicken served with a generous amount of Ryan's home-grown vegetables. After demanding a beer to go with it, Robert ate ravenously without thanking or complimenting his hostess. He sat back and belched loudly when he was done.

Ignoring his uncle's rudeness and wanting answers to the questions seething in his mind, Ryan brought up the subject of the horsebox as soon as he could.

'Well, Nunc,' he said, doing his best to sound like a hayseed and well aware that his uncle would find such a nickname offensive. 'Why trail an empty horsebox all this way? You fixin' to buy yourself a couple of horses on the way home? 'Scuse me but I thought you already had the best horses down south?'

'You're playing with me, Ryan.' Robert gave a thin smile, rocking back in his chair. 'You know very well that I've come to take Hunter's Moon off your hands.'

'Good!' Joanne broke in before Ryan could object. 'The sooner that vicious animal leaves, the better. I can't even stand to look at him — knowing that he's responsible for Peter's death.'

'Oh, Mum, we don't know that.' Weary of this old argument, Ryan felt bound to contradict her. 'Tommy's not in the least bit vicious. I saw what happened myself the first time — something scared him, moving under the water. I don't know what happened the second time. Melia didn't get there in time to see.'

'An unfortunate accident. These things happen,' Robert said smoothly, not wanting them to stray off the point. 'Ill-tempered or not, I'm still interested in that horse.'

'Forget it. He's not bad-tempered and definitely not for sale.'

'Let me finish.' Robert flushed, unused to being so rudely interrupted. Most people listened politely to whatever he had to say. 'I know Pete paid over the odds for him but I'm prepared to give you a small profit to take him off your hands.'

'In your dreams, Nunc. If that's why you're here, you've wasted your time. I'll say it again in case you missed it the first time — our horses are not for sale.'

'Surely that's for your mother to decide.' Robert turned to Joanne smiling, confident of her support.

'No.' Ryan hesitated, not wanting to speak of Joanne's condition and his father's intention to leave him in charge of his stables and horses. 'Mum doesn't understand horses so Dad was going to leave them to me.'

'Was going to?' Robert seized on this loophole. 'So you don't have this in writing? Peter hasn't made a will setting out his wishes and confirming them?'

'I don't know.' For a moment, Ryan felt less than assured. 'Dad was still young. He wasn't expecting to — '

'To die? Of course not. Who does? We like to think we have all the time in the world. So let me be clear on this. If Pete didn't make a will, leaving you in charge of the stables, these business decisions remain with Joanne — who has already said she would like me to take Hunter's Moon.' He finished, clapping his hands together in triumph.

'Mum!' Ryan stared at his mother in desperation, willing her to take his side. 'Dad thought of Tommy as our investment in the future. He'd want us to keep him. You know that.'

'The horse that you think was responsible for his death?' Robert's tone was soft but insistent.

'I don't know — I don't know.' Confused, Joanne looked from one to the other of the two faces staring at her so intently, quite unable to decide.

'Don't stress on it, sweetheart.' Robert

patted her hand until she snatched it away. His tone was placating but to Ryan it sounded like the hiss of a snake. 'You think about it overnight and we'll talk about it after the funeral.'

'Yes, yes. After the funeral,' Joanne murmured. 'Oh, my poor Peter.' And she bent her head to hide the fat tears spilling over and rolling down her cheeks. Tinka growled softly, blaming Robert for being the cause of her sorrow.

Ryan stood up, making no attempt to conceal his contempt for his uncle. 'Don't worry, Mum. This man isn't here because he has any feelings for Dad or for you. He's come here for one reason only — to get his grasping fingers on Hunter's Moon.'

Robert stood up and flushed an even deeper shade of red, making Joanne look up at him in alarm.

'Please stop. Aren't things bad enough already?' she said in a voice thick with tears. 'I can't bear these arguments and fights.'

'Sorry, Joanne.' Robert was first to relax and apologize. 'But your son tries my patience. I came here to offer a reasonable solution to your predicament, only to have it thrown back in my face.'

'There is no predicament. We were quite all right until you came,' Ryan shot back at him.

'Your son is a hothead.' Robert ignored him, speaking to Joanne. 'But if he'll shake hands and reconsider my generous offer, I'm willing to overlook his rudeness — this time.' Robert held out his hand.

'There.' Joanne ventured a watery smile, waiting for her son to accept it and apologize. Instead, he moved away from the table, close to tears himself and shaking his head.

'You might fool my mum, Uncle Robert. She thinks well of everyone.' He ground out the words, almost too breathless with emotion to speak. 'But you certainly don't fool me. I'm going to see to the horses.'

\* \* \*

He didn't speak to his uncle again, although the three of them travelled to the crematorium in the funeral director's car behind the hearse. The driver didn't seem to think it odd that nobody spoke. Joanne wept silently the whole time and wouldn't be comforted, huge tears rolling down her face. She mopped them with a handful of sodden tissues.

There were more people in the tiny chapel than Ryan expected. In death, it seemed that Peter Lanigan enjoyed even more popularity than when he was alive. Joanne paused in the entrance, daunted by the sight of so many people until Ryan took her gently by the hand, encouraging her towards the pew set aside for them. A minister they didn't know, engaged by the funeral directors, performed a brief Anglican service. Joanne was all right until the moment came for Peter's coffin to disappear into the furnace when she stood up and cried out.

'Oh, my poor Peter. I can't bear this. No. No.' And, sobbing hysterically, she would have run towards it if Ryan hadn't caught her, holding her back. Overcome by a fresh storm of tears, she collapsed into his embrace.

Afterwards, finding it impossible to talk to the sobbing Joanne or her son, people spoke to Robert, offering him their condolences instead. Urbane and dry-eyed, he shook the hands of those who were well dressed, inviting them to join him for a drink at the pub. Ryan wanted only to get his mother safely home. With the funeral over, he was hoping that Robert would take the hint and leave. If he never set eyes on his uncle again, it would be too soon.

After seeing his mother home and tucked up in bed with a pill to help her sleep, he decided to call on his father's solicitor, hoping that somehow Peter had found the time to make provision for him to take charge of the stables and horses. He had to wait a while as he had no appointment but, aware of the lad's history, Mr Anderson made a time in his busy schedule to see him. When he heard what Ryan wanted, he shook his head.

'I'm so sorry, Ryan. I wish I had better news for you. Unfortunately, a lot of people put off making these arrangements until it's too late. I'm afraid your father was one of them.'

'So Mum is still — '

'The executor of his original will. I'm afraid so. Yes.'

'But can't you talk to Dr Richards — I'm sure she'd be able to put you straight on the long-term effects of Mum's condition.'

'Yes but these things always take time,' the man said gently, in sympathy with the boy's grief. 'And now — now that your father's gone — why does it seem so important to act on all this immediately?'

Realizing the man couldn't help him and too tired to explain further, Ryan stood up and sighed. 'Thank you, Mr Anderson. I won't take up any more of your time.'

'I'm sorry.' The man stood up to show him to the door. 'I wish I could have been of more help.'

In spite of his nephew's hostile attitude, Robert stayed one more night.

Ryan needed to stock up on provisions for the stables and wanted to see Mike, who would be going to Melbourne soon, but he didn't want to leave his mother alone with his uncle. The man was quite capable of going into her bedroom and shaking her awake.

Trying to wait him out, Robert didn't set off until noon but finally he realized Joanne wasn't going to get up and was forced to leave without seeing her and completing the deal on the horse. Once again, Ryan avoided his uncle's handshake although Robert insisted on having the last word.

'This isn't the last you'll hear of me, boy. One way or another, I always get what I want.'

Ryan smiled, refusing to be intimidated by his uncle's words, and heaved a sigh of relief as he watched Robert leave, the empty horsebox bouncing behind him.

'Has he really gone?' Joanne asked, before venturing from her room.

'Yeah,' Ryan said. 'We finally wore him down. I don't think he'll be back.' He glanced at his watch. 'Will you be OK for an hour or two, Mum? I need to call at the store and order more feed for the horses. Then I want to drop in on Mike. He's leaving to start his training in Melbourne soon.'

'Of course I'll be all right — now Robert

has gone. It'll be nice to have the house to myself for once. I can catch up on my soap — haven't seen it for days.'

'Nothing will have happened. It never does. I've got my phone so just call if you need anything.'

Joanne smiled. 'I'm OK. Go and spend a bit of time with Mike.'

★   ★   ★

As always when he visited the home of Mike's parents, Ryan was reminded of the contrast between the mansion with its Olympic-sized pool and bowling-green lawns and his own more traditional rustic Queensland home. Mike's father was on his way out but he took the time to clap Ryan on the shoulder and once more offer his sympathies.

'Don't be a stranger, Ryan. Always welcome here — you know that.'

Mike was also pleased to see him although he couldn't understand his friend's reluctance to help him deliver another boat.

'Come on, you made excuses last time and missed out on that trip to Whitsundays. This time I won't take no for an answer.'

'Mike, I'd love to but I can't. Mum's not in a good place — she's still pretty fragile — '

'I know but you still need some time for

yourself. After all she's a grown-up, isn't she?'

'Not always.'

'What does that mean?'

Ryan hesitated, wondering if it would be disloyal to tell. 'Hell, you're going to be a doctor — you might as well know.' And putting it as simply as he could, he told his friend about his mother's worsening condition.

'I had no idea or I wouldn't have said what I did.' Mike was considerably chastened and shocked by this news. 'Are you sure there's nothing they can do?'

'Just treat the symptoms as they show up. That's what Dad said. We could have managed together for some time but I'm afraid that sooner rather than later, she'll have to go into care. That's why it's now more important than ever for me to turn Tommy into a successful racehorse. We're going to need more than my veggie patch can provide.'

'But you're only the same age as me. You don't even have a trainer's licence — '

'Not yet. I'll have to make it my business to get one as soon as I can.' Ryan sighed, knowing how hard it would be to plead his cause to the conservative racing authorities. 'But enough about me and my troubles. How are you? What happened about that girl and the baby?'

Mike grinned. 'Oh, that's old news. Either she wasn't pregnant or she lost it, so I'm off the hook.'

'And is she all right?'

'I suppose so.' Mike shrugged. 'I'm done with her, like I told you.'

Ryan stared at his friend, stunned by his lack of compassion. There were times when Mike could be quite insensitive; he could only hope he would use this sense of detachment to make himself a better surgeon, which was his ultimate goal. 'I should go,' he said, glancing at his watch. 'It'll be dark soon and I don't want to leave Mum alone after nightfall.'

'You can't put your life on hold forever. You might be looking for a safe pozzy for her sooner rather than later, bro.'

'Just don't tell anyone, right? Not even your father.'

'I never tell him anything.' Mike grinned and saluted. 'Your secret is safe with me.'

★   ★   ★

Ryan drove home with a lot to think about. He felt a jolt of fear when he saw that the sun had gone down and there were no lights on in the house. He burst through the back door to find his mother sitting at the kitchen table, staring at nothing.

'Mum, what's wrong? What happened? Why are you sitting in the dark?'

'Robert,' she whispered. 'Robert came back.'

'Oh, shit. Of course he did. Why didn't I think of that?' Ryan was so incensed, he didn't realize he was shouting.

'Don't yell at me, Ryan. You know it upsets me.'

'Sorry, sorry.' He sat down beside his mother, taking her hands. 'Just tell me — why did he come back? What did he want?'

'What he wanted all along. To take Tommy.' She pushed a fat envelope towards him. 'He had the money all ready and paid me in cash. I haven't counted it but there seems to be an awful lot — '

'Oh, Mum. Why didn't you call me? I'd have come home.'

'I don't know. He was so kind to me, so sympathetic — not how he was with you. He said he could see I needed the money to fix up the house.'

Ryan closed his eyes. His uncle had been clever. He had picked on the very thing closest to Joanne's heart. 'And Tommy's papers — did he take them, too?' He glanced at his father's desk, hating the thought of his uncle rummaging through it to find them.

'And how long ago did he leave?' He held out his hand for the envelope when she would have snatched it away. 'No, Mum, give it to me. I might catch up with him yet.'

'Ryan, it's too late. It's done. You'll only argue with him and make him angry again.'

'He hasn't seen angry yet. Taking advantage of a grieving woman who isn't — '

'Quite right in the head? Oh, don't worry — I know what people say about me.'

'Oh, Mum.' Ryan picked up the envelope and tucked it into his jacket. Sometimes he wished she didn't have these moments of perception. 'Just tell me how long? How long ago did he leave?'

'I don't know. Two hours. Maybe three.'

'Well, he can't travel fast with a horse in a box. I could catch up with him yet.'

'Now, Ryan, please. Don't do anything foolish.'

'Don't worry. If he's three hours ahead of me, I'll have plenty of time to calm down.'

Driving as fast as he could and sometimes over the speed limits, Ryan kept an eye out for police cars as he lane-hopped, dodging in and out of the traffic on the highway. Even at night it wasn't long before he spotted his uncle's distinctive trailer with Lanigan's Melbourne in flashy luminous letters on the back and sides. Although he was well past

Cairns, he hadn't covered nearly as much ground as Ryan expected. Fuelled by anger and frustration, he drove in front of Robert quite dangerously, forcing him to stop at the side of the road. Robert jumped out of his car and ran towards him, equally angry.

'What's the matter with you, boy, forcing me off the road at night. You tryin' to get us both killed?'

'Here's your filthy money.' Ryan flung the envelope at Robert's feet. 'Now give me the horse you stole.'

'How? You figurin' on tyin' him to the back of your car an' makin' him trot home?' Robert mocked his nephew, ignoring the packet lying on the road between them. 'I haven't stolen anything. I paid for that animal fair an' square. Best get back home to your momma, son. I don't think she does too well on her own.'

But Ryan wasn't listening, already running to the horsebox to check on Tommy. Even before he opened it, he knew there would be no horse inside.

'Where is he? What have you done with — ' he started to say.

Robert laughed shortly. 'Think I'm a fool, boy? I knew you'd be hot on my trail soon as you found me out. You're too late. I sent Hunter's Moon off in luxury not half an hour ago. Look up an' you'll probably see the lights of that silver bird right there in the sky. My man's goin' to meet him at the airport. Hunter's Moon will be home and hosed long before I get there.'

'You — you bastard,' Ryan said, realizing his uncle had outsmarted and beaten him.

'Yeah, well. I've been called worse.' He pointed to the packet of money, lying on the ground. 'Better pick that up, boy. Your momma's goin' to need it. I won't say I'm hopin' to see you any time soon.' So saying, he gave a mocking salute, climbed back into his vehicle and drove away, leaving Ryan in a cloud of dust at the side of the road. Ryan picked up the discarded envelope and brushed the soil from it, watching him go. Back in his car, for the first time he unfastened the envelope, looked at the money and counted it. His uncle had given them the exact amount his father had paid for Hunter's Moon.

# 4

Robert took his time on the return journey, feeling happier than he had in days. From time to time he let out a bellow of laughter, pleased with himself for acquiring the horse he had wanted for so long and with the added bonus of getting the better of his nephew. He had enjoyed seeing the dejected slump of the young man's shoulders when he realized he was defeated; it made all his plotting worthwhile. His foreman in Melbourne had already texted him to say that Hunter's Moon had arrived safely and was settling into his new quarters as if he had been there all his life. As a precaution, he had called the vet, who examined him thoroughly, pronouncing him fit, in spite of the fact that he had been living and exercising in what Robert described as relatively primitive conditions.

Delighted that he had accomplished his goal more easily than he had expected, he decided to make a detour to Sydney to give himself a small reward. There was a woman he sometimes visited when he was there on his own. It would be wrong to call her a prostitute but in return for good food and expensive presents, she was generous to a select group of men friends. Sensibly he decided to call before arriving on her doorstep unannounced.

'Why, Robert, what a pleasant surprise.' She did indeed sound genuinely pleased to hear from him. 'I love to see you when you're in town. Come over right away. I'll put some champagne on ice.'

Driving down unfamiliar roads, looking out for a flower shop and anticipating the good time he was about to have, Robert ignored a red light. He knew something was wrong only when he heard the noise of air brakes applied far too late and the frantic blaring of a semi-trailer's horn. Had he been driving the car on its own, he might have got away with it, but the horsebox took the full impact of the collision, making the car swing around and crash into the truck. His last thought before blacking out was that he wouldn't get to see Meriel after all.

* * *

It was Chrissie who took the call from the hospital in Sydney, relaying the message to Val.

'But what on earth was he doing in Sydney?' This was her mother's first reaction before she realized that her husband could be in real danger.

'He's been involved in an accident, Mum, and they don't know how serious it is. We'll have to go up there at once. He hasn't come round yet and he's still in intensive care.'

'My God. I didn't realize. I thought it was just a minor bump in the car. He is going to be all right?' Val was finding it hard to believe such a thing could happen to her seemingly indestructible husband.

'We won't know the whole story till we get there.'

'Well, obviously you can't go. You've enough to do here with the wedding coming up — '

Chrissie shrugged. 'I dunno. Until we know what's happening with Dad, we might have to postpone it.'

'Don't say that. You've the honeymoon booked. It'll upset all of your plans.'

At that point, it didn't occur to either of them that Robert's condition could be critical and that he might die. This was only brought home to Valerie when she walked into the ward to find her husband unconscious and hooked up to various instruments monitoring his condition and with a nurse assigned to his sole care. A tall, severe-looking woman with her hair scraped back from her face, she was busy making notes on his chart.

'He — um — he will be all right, won't he?' Val asked.

'Hard to say. We'll know more if and when he regains consciousness.' The nurse took down some more notes from the instruments beside the bed. 'The police will want to talk to him then. The truck driver says your husband drove through a red light.'

Val stared at her. 'I don't know what he was doing in Sydney. He was supposed to be on the highway, coming home.'

The nurse shrugged. 'We see this sort of thing all the time. People distracted, talking on mobile phones.'

'How do you know he was on the phone?'

'It was still in his hand. Look, I shouldn't be discussing this. It's a matter for the police. The truck driver was pretty shaken up, too.'

It occurred to Val that there was a lot more sympathy for the truck driver than for her husband's plight. She booked into a cheap motel not far from the hospital and reported the news — or rather the lack of it — to Chrissie.

'Stay just as long as you need to, Mum. And don't worry about things here. Sam and Bill can take care of the horses — for the time being, anyway. I'm going into town to see Tony tomorrow to give him the heads-up that we might have to postpone — '

'Oh, Chrissie. I hope it won't come to that.'

On reflection, Chrissie was surprised to find out how little she cared. It had been several weeks since she had seen Tony, who had given up calling her every night as he used to do. She had the feeling he was beginning to take her for granted.

At the end of twenty-four hours, Robert regained consciousness but he seemed vague, having no memory of the accident or how it occurred. He seemed surprised to see Val and wondered why she was there. His doctors told her that while his injuries seemed to be relatively minor, the horsebox taking the main impact of the collision, the shock of the accident had caused him to suffer a minor stroke. And although they expected him to make a reasonable recovery, he would be confined to a wheelchair in the immediate future. His medical insurance would cover the cost of an ambulance to deliver him back to Melbourne where his own doctor would take over, referring him to a specialist who would monitor his progress. It was suggested that Val should consider hiring a nurse. She reported all this to Chrissie, who sighed.

'I've already talked to Tony and arranged to see him tomorrow. Looks as if we'll need to rethink our plans.'

'Really? You don't sound all that put out.'

'Don't I?' Chrissie sounded flat. 'I'll know more after I've spoken to Tony.'

★   ★   ★

As she drove into town the next day, Chrissie had time to consider her relationship with her fiancé and how it had changed. Having met him in college, he was her first love and she had assumed she would love him forever, although the excitement seemed to have gone out of the relationship in recent times.

They had been best friends long before they became lovers. She had always been the smart one, lending him her notes and letting him copy her work. At one time she was even accused of copying his, but eventually the truth came out when Tony couldn't help revealing his lack of application and he was politely advised to leave. Even then, Chrissie remained loyal, doing her best to 'stand by her man' while he made a new beginning in the hospitality industry. This suited him better as he had the knack of charming people to do things for him all the time.

If Chrissie was wearing her reading glasses when he wanted to kiss her, he used to take them off and say she was beautiful. She had believed him, too, and was thrilled when he asked her to marry him although other people — mostly girls — said he was unreliable as well as being a serious gambler, too. He had been seen playing poker not just at the casino but at some of the less well-regulated clubs. Chrissie dismissed these rumours as founded in jealousy, although she did know about his gambling and had sometimes helped out, paying his debts. He always promised it wouldn't happen again — until the next time.

After the wedding, they were planning an extended trip to London and Paris. There weren't many girls who could boast of a honeymoon in Paris, the city of romance. But now, because of the news about Robert, these plans were all up in the air. And, even if Val hired a full-time nurse, Chrissie knew she couldn't leave her mother to cope alone with a man who was sure to be the most overbearing and demanding of patients.

Chrissie had arranged to meet Tony for lunch at the hotel where he worked on probation as an assistant manager. It was one of the newer ones at the top end of town, patronized by politicians and show-business celebrities.

She knew something was wrong as soon as she saw him coming towards her. He was handsome as ever, well groomed and his blond hair gleaming, but he seemed to have lost weight since she last saw him and his smile was strained, a small muscle twitching beneath his eye. As a rule, Tony sailed through life on a golden cloud, never letting anything trouble him. He was the prince of charm and took it for granted that everyone loved him. He could have the grumpiest of hotel guests eating out of his hand in moments.

She moved into his arms and raised her lips for his kiss but he pushed her away with a brief peck on the cheek before steering her towards the dining room and the private alcove where they were to dine. She tipped her head to one side, considering him.

'Come on, Tony, I know that look,' she said. 'What is it this time? Not losing at poker again, I hope?'

'Oh, Chrissie.' He glanced aside, looking mildly irritated. 'You know very well I've given that up.' And he hid his expression by picking up the menu, giving his full attention to that instead.

'What will you have?' he said from behind it. 'The chef's doing fresh crayfish today and I hear that it's good.'

While pretending to study the menu herself, Chrissie felt someone's stare and looked up to catch the eye of a slender blonde who was serving behind the bar. She had that smooth, heavy hair that fell forward on either side of her face; the kind of hairstyle that looks simple but can take half an hour to prepare. She looked away as soon as she realized Chrissie had seen her, a faint blush staining her cheeks.

'Crayfish would be great,' Chrissie said, snapping the menu shut. 'But first things first. I wanted to ask if you've given your notice yet?'

'Actually, I haven't.' Tony bit his lip, once more failing to meet her gaze.

'Good,' she said, making him blink in surprise. Briefly, she gave him an outline of what had happened to Robert and apologized for delaying their wedding plans. 'It won't be forever,' she concluded. 'Just until we find out how he's going to be.'

'Right,' he murmured, staring at her. She could tell he was more immersed in his own thoughts than in what she had to say. 'Sorry to hear about your pa,' he mumbled almost as an afterthought.

'Where are you, Tony?' She sat back, regarding him. 'I can see you're not here with me.'

'No. Yes. Sorry, sorry.'

She closed her eyes, trying to contain her impatience. 'Tony, will you please stop saying 'sorry' and give me your full attention.'

'Yes. Chrissie, I'm sorry.' The words came out in a rush. 'I feel awful doing this to you when you've got so much else on your plate. But I can't marry you. Nor can I leave my job and take off for Europe — not now or any time soon. I'd be giving up too much here.'

'I see.' She paused, wondering about this sudden turn-around. After all, he was the one who had suggested the overseas trip. 'OK. Maybe it's for the best in view of what's happened. I'll tell them at work about these changed plans.'

'Yeah.' He looked considerably relieved. 'You do that. And thanks. Thanks for taking it all so well.'

'I don't know so much about that,' Chrissie said, surprised and a little hurt that he should fall in with her suggestion so easily. Did he really not care?

She became more and more aware of somebody watching them. The blonde behind the bar was now staring openly, making no attempt to disguise her interest. Chrissie turned in her seat to look at her directly but immediately the girl looked away, pretending to wipe the bar.

'Who is that girl, Tony?' she said. 'And why is she so interested in us?'

'That's Alison,' he mumbled, refusing to look at her. 'She's new.'

'Doesn't she know that it's rude to stare?'

'Oh, Chrissie, I'm so sorry.' He sat back in his seat, looking defeated. 'I feel such a heel when you've been so wonderful to me always.' He reached across the table, trying to grab her hands, but she snatched them back out of the way. 'I really hate letting you down, especially at a time like this, but I can't help it. I've fallen in love. Really in love this time.'

'Yeah. With that blonde airhead over there.'

His surprise was almost comical. 'How did you guess?'

'Because I'm psychic, you idiot.' At that moment, Chrissie was too angry to feel any pain. 'And I'm not hungry just now. So if it's all the same to you, I think I'll pass on lunch.' Feeling a buzzing in her ears, she stood up to leave, wanting to put as much distance between them as she could.

'Chrissie, please.' Tony stood up. 'We have so much history together. Let's behave like civilized people. Please stay and have lunch as we planned. I don't want us to part bad friends.'

'That's just it, Tony, isn't it?' She looked at this handsome, spoilt young man as if seeing him properly for the first time. She took off her engagement ring and pushed it towards him. 'We've always had an uneven relation-ship. I give — you take — and I don't think we've ever really been friends.'

She left the table with her head high, knowing it was unlikely that she would ever see him again. He was probably already cracking a bottle of champagne, celebrating his freedom with his new love. She wondered, rather unkindly, how the new girl would feel when he asked her to help him to pay for his gambling debts. When her initial indignation subsided, she was surprised to find she wasn't as upset as she expected to be. She was her own woman again — she was free. Tony was a luxury she no longer needed to afford. As she took the road home towards Cranbourne, she put on a new CD and sang along with it, enjoying a sense of freedom and independence, feeling more light-hearted than she had in years.

# 5

The wind was already howling around the house, gusting strongly enough to make the windows rattle. The sound was disturbing and, with increasing apprehension, Ryan listened to the latest news bulletins on the radio warning people that an intense tropical cyclone was heading for the coast of North Queensland and that it was unlikely to miss. More often than not, a cyclone would veer off out to sea or lose intensity before hitting the mainland, but not this time. Even the newsreader sounded tense and on the verge of panic.

'Residents are urged to head for the Evacuation Centres without delay. The weather bureau cannot advise exactly when the storm will hit but no one should be caught out-doors, as flying debris will be the least of your troubles — '

He realized he should have woken her earlier and left home before.

'Mum.' He crouched beside her chair, shaking her gently so as not to alarm her. 'Wake up. We really do have to leave now — we should have gone hours ago.'

'What for?' Joanne awoke with a start, looking bleary-eyed. 'I don't want to be caught outside if it's going to rain. And if we leave now, I'll miss my favourite soap.' She sounded petulant as a child. 'Rose's daughter is getting married this week and you know how I've been looking forward to it — '

Ryan closed his eyes, praying for patience. 'It's just a story, Mum. Those people aren't real.'

'Not to you maybe.' Joanne's lip trembled and her face fell into sulky lines. 'They're like family to me.'

Ryan said nothing, suppressing the angry response that would only make her cry. If she were upset, it would be that much harder to get her to move. He glanced around the room, checking that he'd done as much as he could to make everything secure. He had pushed the dining chairs under the table and tied all their legs together so that nothing would move and pushed the larger pieces of furniture back against the walls. Everything that would fit had been stuffed into chests and the drawers taped shut. He had already turned off the power, knowing the electricity company would be closing it down at the mains.

While Joanne was sitting there sleeping, with her little dog in her lap, Ryan had been busy making the house secure, taping all the windows to stop them from shattering in the expected high winds. He could only hope that this old weatherboard home, built on stilts like most traditional Queenslanders', would be capable of withstanding the worst of storms.

Joanne continued to stare at the blank television set, willing it to come back to life and entertain her.

'Mum!' Ryan tried again. 'The electricity's off, anyway. We must go now or we won't get to the Evacuation Centre in time. Once it's locked down, they won't open up for anything and the storm's on its way. It will be here quite soon.'

'I don't care.' She pouted like a child, angry about missing her show. 'And anyway, you're just a boy. It's not your business to tell me what to do.' She drew herself up and looked down her nose at him; a new habit she had developed when she wanted to pull rank. 'I'll leave when I'm good and ready and not before.'

'Oh, Mum.' He sighed. 'Please don't be difficult. Not now.'

'I dunno what all the fuss is about. We've seen storms before — it's a hazard of living here. It'll be a bit of a blow, that's all.' She smiled up at him, abnormally serene. 'Look at you, darling. Getting all hot and bothered over nothing. Anyone would think we're about to face World War Three.'

'I don't have time for this, Mum. I don't want to scare you but right now there's a storm heading this way and it'll be a lot more than just a blow. A full-blown cyclone, category four and gathering momentum even as we speak. It's massive and nobody knows what will happen when it hits. It will be stronger, larger and wider than anything we've seen before.'

'So what?' His mother was still unimpressed. 'It is February, after all. The wet season. Storms are to be expected at this time of year.'

'Not like this one. Don't you see how quiet it is out there? Can you hear any birds?'

'No.'

'That's because they've all left. Birds and other wild creatures sense these changes in the weather. They know when it's not safe to stay.'

'You go on then, Ryan.' She smiled serenely and patted his hand, making him wonder if it had been a mistake to let her take two of her sedative pills instead of the usual one. 'I'll be OK. I'll just sit here with Tinka and wait till your father gets home.'

Ryan didn't know what to say. Although

Peter's funeral had taken place some months ago now, Joanne was still in denial concerning his death. She refused to believe he wasn't away on some errand in town. Her short-term memory was already failing and, as Doctor Richards predicted, she was going downhill fast. Only in her mid-forties, she was already losing her grip on reality, reverting to childhood. Her closest companion was Tinka, the little Italian greyhound who was sitting beside her now, pressing against her legs. Tinka, who had sense enough to shiver in apprehension, aware of the storm that was on its way.

Ryan smiled at the little dog, which looked back at him with trusting eyes. He still hadn't found a way to tell Joanne that Tinka wouldn't be allowed into the Evacuation Centre. The woman in charge there had been adamant when the question was raised.

'Of course you can't bring a dog,' she snapped. 'This refuge is only for people. It will be crowded enough as it is without the stink of animals, too. You and your mother should get here as soon as you can.' The woman's voice trembled and Ryan sensed she was holding herself together with some effort. 'And do hurry! The latest reports say the storm is headed for Canesville directly. You're right in the path of it.'

Ryan knew then it would be useless to say that his mother's security depended on that little dog. Her sanity even. Somehow, he'd have to get Joanne into the ute without Tinka, then make an excuse to run back and shut the little dog in with the fowls. He couldn't think what else to do. All hell would break loose when Joanne realized the little dog had been left behind. He could only hope she wouldn't try to get out of the car.

Joanne dithered, taking an age to locate her purse, and then she said she couldn't find Tinka's lead. This was when Ryan knew it was too late to go anywhere. The winds were already rising and it would be fatal to be caught out of doors. They must resort to plan B, taking the portable radio into the bathroom and hiding themselves under mattresses for protection. Hopefully, the old weatherboard home could withstand the storm and the torrential rain and floods that must follow.

'What are you doing?' Joanne complained as she watched her son strip the beds and stagger with the mattresses, forcing them into the bathroom. 'I thought you said we had to leave now?'

'Too late.' He was grunting with the effort of heaving the two queen-sized mattresses through the narrow doorway, one after the other. After that, he gathered as many blankets and pillows as he could find. It all proved to be a tight fit, which was no bad thing. 'We're stopping here after all.'

'Be careful with my mattress. It's almost new,' Joanne complained. 'And it'll be too hot. We could suffocate in there.'

Ignoring her string of complaints, Ryan grabbed some bottles of water, packets of biscuits and the bags that had been packed to go to the Evacuation Centre. He had boiled a kettle earlier and filled a thermos flask with hot tea. Also he checked the strongest flashlight and located some spare batteries. The electricity could be off for some time.

'Right. That ought to see us through in the short term.' He smiled brightly at his mother to reassure her. 'In you go then, with Tinka. We'll be nice and snug.'

'I don't want to. It'll be awfully cramped and I won't be able to breathe,' Joanne grumbled as she stood in the doorway to the bathroom, watching as Ryan bolted the back door. 'And I still think we should wait for your father.'

'Mum, will you stop it?' Finally Ryan's nerve snapped. 'Stop torturing yourself and me. Get it through your head that Dad's not coming back. He died months ago.'

'What a wicked thing to say!' Before he

realized what she would do, she stepped forward and slapped him across the face with the full force of her arm behind it. 'You know where he is. Away at the show. Getting new equipment for the farm.'

'The show?' Ryan massaged his flaming cheek. 'You think so, really? At this time of year?'

At last the meaning of his words sank in and she clasped both hands to her mouth, eyes wide with shock. Being forced to remember the truth knocked all the fight out of her and she allowed Ryan to push her into the bathroom and make her comfortable on a beanbag with the mattress tucked around and over her, Tinka at her feet. 'Oh, my poor Peter,' she murmured through trembling lips. 'How could I forget?'

'It's OK, Mum.' Ryan hugged her, feeling mean for forcing her to remember when he knew how emotionally fragile she was. But he was scared, too, and his patience had been tried to the limit. 'We'll be all right. We just have to get through tonight.'

Already the wind was howling through the trees, ripping off branches and shredding the leaves. There was a lot of banging outside as anything not tied down out of doors was getting blown around. It sounded as if a giant had lost his temper out there. The rain clattered on the tin roof, making it impossible to speak, which was no bad thing. Ryan pulled the mattresses closer as the wind screamed around the house like an angry demon. He couldn't be sure how long it went on but it felt like forever until, just as suddenly as it had started, all the noise stopped, followed by an equally eerie silence.

'There, what did I tell you?' Joanne gave a nervous giggle as she pushed the mattress aside and struggled to her feet. 'It's over, thank God, and the house still standing. I must let Tinka out, she'll want to pee.'

'Mum, wait, the storm's not over yet. It's only quiet because we're in the eye.'

But she was already urging the little dog towards the back door. She drew back the bolt and opened it before Ryan could stop her. He expected it to be torn from its hinges and his mother whirled aside by the force of the storm. Instead, all was quiet and still out there.

Tinka rushed outside and squatted quickly. She understood that she shouldn't waste time. She finished what she needed to do and ran back to Ryan, tongue lolling. Absent-mindedly, he patted her.

But Joanne was in no hurry to come in and remained staring up at the sky in wonderment, arms outstretched. 'Oh, Ryan, do look at the sky, how clear the night is. I've never seen so many stars. It's as if you can look right through them all to see God in his heaven.'

'Mum, please come back inside. The storm isn't over yet.'

'Don't be such an old woman, Ryan. You worry too much. It's just as I said — a big ole fuss about nothing. People give in to panic too easily.'

Ryan thought this a bit rich, coming from a woman who had a screaming fit if she saw a big spider, but said nothing, relieved to draw her back into the house.

The wind was already building from another direction this time and it wasn't long before the storm was raging again, ten times worse than before. The wind screamed around them, venting its fury with a sound like several freight trains on a collision course. Then there was a loud noise like a bomb going off as if some flying debris had punched a hole in the other side of the house. Joanne was crying in earnest now, finally believing that they were in serious trouble.

'What are we to do? We'll be killed,' she wailed, clasping Tinka to her bosom as the little dog whimpered, her whole body trembling with fear.

'Stay put. We're as safe in here as we'd be

anywhere.' Ryan wanted to sound calm and reassuring but he wasn't sure Joanne could hear him over the fury of the cyclone. He was beginning to think the house might be torn from its stumps, leaving them vulnerable to the intensity of the storm. Exposed to the elements, they would face certain death.

Finally, although it was still pouring with rain, the winds gradually dropped and, against all odds, Joanne fell asleep. In the early hours of the morning, Ryan switched on the radio in the hope of hearing some news. It took a while to come through, none of it good. Throughout the district, there had been massive damage to property and all the banana plantations and cane fields were laid waste. Farmers would have to start all over again. Miraculously, so far there was no news that anyone had been killed. Although there were strict instructions coming through on the radio that no one should venture out of doors, Joanne refused to stay put in the bathroom and, when it had been quiet for some time, they both went outside to assess the damage to the house. Even before seeing the full extent of it, Ryan knew they wouldn't be able to live there as it was.

Great holes had been punched in the far side and half the roof had been torn away. Sheets of corrugated iron lay scattered all over the yard and what had once been Ryan's vegetable garden was drowning in rain and mud. Their livelihood was no more. The shed that had housed the chickens had completely disappeared, along with the occupants; just a few feathers remained.

'Mum! Come back to the house!' Ryan called from the doorway, trying to stop her, but she was already running towards the empty space, her fist in her mouth.

'My little friends! Who has stolen our chickens? Where have they gone?'

There weren't many big trees on the property. Some time ago when things were tight, Peter had sold a big cedar to a furniture maker, leaving just a few eucalypts, not known for their stability at the best of times. One was already down, the roots torn from the ground, and Joanne was standing quite close to the other one.

Suddenly, there was a loud crack like a big gun going off and a huge branch fell, giving Ryan no time to shout a warning. He could only stare as it settled over the spot where Joanne had been standing just a moment before. For a moment or so, like a fool, he wondered where she'd gone. It was only when Tinka raised her head and started to howl that he realized she had been crushed underneath it. She wouldn't have known what hit her. Blood was already starting to pool, mingling with the rain and mud on the ground. And, even before he screwed up the courage to take a closer look, he knew there was no possibility his mother could have survived.

# 6

It looked as if Joanne's funeral would be poorly attended. The little town was still reeling from the devastation left in the wake of the cyclone. Many local people were crowded in with relatives and friends as their own homes had been damaged or destroyed. Among this number was Ryan, who now had to deal with much more than the loss of his mother. The roof had been torn off the house, leaving it exposed to the elements, and his once nourishing market garden had been reduced to a mess of broken plants and mud, his livelihood gone. And, worst of all, Sprite appeared to have taken fright and run away.

Aside from the money Robert had paid for Tommy and which Ryan was trying to leave untouched, there was just enough left from their dwindling resources to pay for Joanne's funeral. Needing to find a positive somewhere, he allowed himself to hope that after all the misery he had suffered, as well as the loss of his parents, Robert might now relent sufficiently to let him buy the horse back. Slim as it was, he had to believe in this possibility or the future looked bleak indeed.

Rebuilding the house was another matter entirely. Had Joanne survived, he would have been obliged to forget about Tommy and spend whatever money they had on repairing their home. It was no surprise to find that his parents had no household or building insurance to cover these needs. Concerned only with the well-being of his horses and uninterested in practical matters or keeping proper accounts, Peter had allowed the household policies to lapse. In any case, there were usually clauses somewhere in the fine print to protect the company against 'natural disasters' such as this. Acts of God, they liked to call them — more like Acts of the Devil, Ryan thought.

On top of everything else, he had the added heartbreak of losing Sprite. Although the solid brick stable block had survived the storm, all the doors had been blown off their hinges and the terrified horse had run off. Following advice he had gleaned from the internet, he had hung a strap with his mobile phone number and address around the horse's neck but after several days of fruitless enquiries, he had been forced to give up hope. In any case, without the means to recharge it, his mobile had turned itself off. He needed to find someone with power to get it started again.

It occurred to him that he had no one but himself to think about now and experienced a measure of guilty relief about this.

Mike's father invited him to come and stay while he made up his mind what to do. Glen Harrison had turned up as soon as the roads were clear, finding Ryan in the process of moving what he could salvage into the empty stable block to create a makeshift home for himself.

Glen stared around, appalled by the thought of anyone attempting to carry on under such conditions.

'You can't possibly live out here, lad, it's quite primitive. You'll catch your death.'

'I can't leave, Mr Harrison. Sprite has been missing since the night of the storm and I have to wait and see if she can make her way back.'

'Ah.' Mike's father stared at the ground for a moment, knowing he was about to heap more bad news on a lad who had already suffered enough. 'We found the bodies of several horses caught in the river; it was moving too rapidly for them to swim and they must have drowned.'

'That's OK. If there was more than one horse, it wouldn't be Sprite. She was alone.'

'No.' Glen hesitated before going on. 'It was almost washed out but the remains of your notice was still tied around her neck, caught in the debris. We could see she was a thoroughbred rather than an ordinary pony but they had to bury her along with the others — it couldn't wait.'

This last news was too much for Ryan, who broke into painful, gasping tears. 'S-sorry,' he said, fighting to gain control as the older man awkwardly patted him on the shoulder. 'But — but, poor Sprite — after everything else — it's too much.' He had to stop, his throat tightening with renewed grief.

'Ryan, I know you can't think past your mother's funeral but in the short term you're coming to stay with us. I know Mike would want us to look after you.'

'It's good of you, Mr Harrison, but I'll stay here. I'd rather not be a burden to anyone.' Really, Ryan wanted to stay where he was, retaining his independence and making his own decisions. He didn't want to be 'taken over' by Mike's father.

'You won't be a burden. You'll be most welcome.'

'But what about Mrs — um — she might not like it?'

'Don't you worry about Fiona — I'll square things with her.' Glen clapped the young man on the shoulder, heartily enough to make him wince. 'Go on. Pick up a few essentials and come with me now.'

'I don't have much to bring — only Tinka, Mum's little dog. Bit miserable, I'm afraid, as she doesn't know what's happening. She was very much Mum's dog.'

'Fiona's marvellous with dogs. She'll take care of it.'

Ryan attempted a smile, wondering if Fiona would mind living up to all these promises being made on her behalf. He didn't have to wonder for long.

★   ★   ★

On arrival at the Harrisons' place, he could see they'd been lucky. Somehow Glen's property had been spared the worst of the storm. A couple of pool boys were already scooping the leaves and debris from the pool and hosing down the loungers which had been tossed around by the storm. A team of gardeners had been employed to clear up the wreckage, setting the flower beds to rights. Inside, the house was very much as Ryan remembered it; he could see no evidence of storm damage. Since the property had its own generator in case of emergency, they had suffered no loss of facilities at all.

They came in to the family room to find Fiona in the midst of a conversation on her mobile phone. She waved briefly to Glen and gave him a tight smile before she continued.

'Yes, I do see where you're coming from, Mr Mayor. Glen does have a home largely untouched by storm damage. And you should know we're doing our bit. We've already taken in the Lanigan boy so there's no way we can take in any more orphans of the storm.'

Ryan experienced a flash of annoyance that she was making him the excuse for not accommodating anyone else. On top of that, she spoke of him as if he were a helpless child when, in fact, he had taken care of his mother since his father died and, if Mike's father hadn't insisted, he would much rather have stayed at home.

She listened to what the mayor was saying and Ryan could see she was becoming irritated, two spots of colour appearing high on her cheekbones. 'Yes, indeed. We might well have enough room and beds to accommodate six more people but we just don't have the facilities or the manpower to look after them. Selfishness doesn't come into it.'

The mayor must have had a lot more to say on the subject of selfishness but Fiona withdrew from the conversation, cutting him short. 'I'm sorry but things are extremely hectic here at present. Trust me. I'll get back to you as soon as I can offer you something more.'

The mayor wasn't prepared to let it go at that; Fiona's dark eyes flashed and her nostrils flared as she listened to further criticism. To Ryan, she seemed a dragon lady indeed.

'I said I'll get back to you.' She ground out the words. 'And I'm not in the habit of lying.' Her expression softened as she caught sight of Tinka, who was cringing in Ryan's arms, daunted to find herself in unfamiliar surroundings.

'Oh, what a sweet little dog. Come to me, darling.' She held out her hands as Tinka scrabbled to reach her. 'And what's your name?'

'It's Tinka,' Ryan murmured, irritated that the little dog should transfer her affections so easily. 'She was my mother's dog.'

'Poor sweetheart.' Fiona dropped a kiss on her head, receiving a good licking in return. It occurred to Ryan that Fiona had far more compassion for this little bereaved animal than for any human being left destitute after the storm.

He knew it was unwise to make snap judgements but he disliked the woman intensely, although he had not met her before. Dressed in tennis clothes that showed off her elegant, spray-tanned legs and well-toned body, she looked as if she had suffered no hardship from the storm. Her glamour was stranded in the late eighties with a mane of brittle, blonde hair teased out of existence and heavily lacquered to keep it in place. She wore a luminous pink lipstick that might have flattered her as a teenager but now only emphasized her thin lips and her eyelids were painted a startling, electric blue, the sparse lashes liberally coated with mascara to match.

Glen Harrison took just a moment to introduce them and made himself scarce, going outside to confer with his gardeners.

'You should know it wasn't my idea to come here,' Ryan said at once, folding his arms. 'I was perfectly all right where I was.'

'Glen didn't think so,' she said shortly. 'In any case, you won't be here for long. You should be with family at a time like this. I told Mike to get in touch with your people down south.'

'No!' This came out as a wail of anguish. 'You should have asked me first. I don't get on with my family down south.'

'Now isn't the time to hold on to petty disagreements,' Fiona said, dismissing his argument as she fondled the little dog's ears. 'In any case, the dynamic has changed down there. Your uncle had some sort of road accident and he's in a wheelchair now.'

'A wheelchair?' Ryan echoed, stunned by this news.

'Yes, well. They can probably do with your help. Your aunt insists on coming up for your mother's funeral so I've told her she'll be very welcome to stay here.'

'Is that so?' The words fell out before Ryan could stop them. 'You're a piece of work, aren't you? Got it all sorted without asking anyone.'

'I wasn't an office manager for nothing.' Fiona smiled thinly, taking this as a compliment as she patted her helmet of hair. 'A problem solver from way back.'

'And who the hell asked you to solve my problems?' Finally, Ryan lost his temper; the woman's smug satisfaction was too much to bear.

Glen returned in time to catch this last exchange.

'That's a bit much, Ryan,' he said. 'Fiona's only trying to help.'

'Sure. The way she's helping the mayor accommodate the poor, homeless people of Canesville.'

Fiona spoke softly and reasonably, making him seem even more like a bully and a boor. 'Really, Ryan. We can't have Glen's lovely home turned into a bear garden, can we?'

'I think you should both calm down.' Glen made a placating movement with both hands. 'Ryan has lost everything and is understandably upset. And you, Fiona — you need to cut him some slack.'

Ryan said nothing but he made his attitude clear by reclaiming Tinka, who sprang into his embrace, grateful to get away from Fiona's cloying perfume that was making her sneeze. But Fiona was determined to have the last word as she headed for the door.

'I do hope that dog's house-trained. There's an old kennel outside she can live in, if not.'

'Take no notice of Fee,' Glen said when she was gone. 'Her bark is a whole lot worse than her bite.'

Ryan disagreed but he couldn't say so. His mind was racing as he considered this piece of news Fiona had dropped on him so casually. Robert Lanigan was facing life in a wheelchair. What did that mean? Was this a temporary setback or was he permanently crippled? He found he was actually looking forward to his aunt's arrival to find out. He could only hope that, as a woman of the same generation, she wouldn't be anything like Fiona.

★   ★   ★

She wasn't. Valerie Lanigan wore little make-up and was dressed in casual trousers and practical, everyday clothes. She struck him immediately as a warm-hearted, motherly person and, best of all, she was not in the least like Fiona.

As his own elderly ute had fallen victim to the storm, Glen allowed him to borrow a car to fetch her from the airport at Cairns. He also thought it would be a good opportunity for them to get to know one another before the funeral and without interference from anyone else.

He held up a notice, scanning the crowd from the newly arrived plane bringing those who had come to rescue relatives or help clean up the storm damage. He identified her almost at once — a plump woman in her late forties, looking small and shy as if she wasn't accustomed to travelling alone. She smiled with relief when she saw him, dropping her travelling bag to enfold him in a warm embrace.

'You must be Ryan,' she said simply. 'I'd know you anywhere — you look just like your mother.'

This unexpected kindness brought tears to Ryan's eyes and he gasped, holding them in.

'Oh, my dear, I'm so clumsy. I shouldn't have said that.' Valerie hugged him again.

'The last thing I want to do is upset you.'

'It's OK. I should say 'Welcome to Queensland' but there isn't much to welcome you to just now,' Ryan managed to say through the tightness in his throat.

He settled Valerie in the front seat and they drove north. She wasn't a chatterbox but from time to time she exclaimed at the devastation left by the storm — mile after mile of cane fields lying steaming and rotting under the sun and banana plantations flattened to the ground.

'I had no idea,' she said. 'We saw newsreels and pictures on television but nobody realized it was as bad as this. Can they recover?'

'Probably,' Ryan said. 'Tropical plants grow up quickly and we're a tough breed up here.'

'I wasn't going to talk to you about making plans right away but I feel differently now that I'm here. I came first of all to support you through the funeral. But I'm hoping you'll see your way clear to coming down south and making a home with us.'

'That's very kind, Aunt Val — but I really don't think that's a good idea.'

'Just call me Val — everyone does.'

'Look, I don't want to be rude or throw your kindness back in your face but I can't do that. I can't live in the same house as your

101

husband when he took advantage of my mother's naivety, tricking her into selling him my father's best horse.'

'Yes, I know. I did hear something about that — '

'It's not an easy thing for me to set aside and forget. And just by being there, I'd be a constant thorn in your husband's side.'

'You say this because you remember the Robert who was. He's sadly diminished these days; a shadow of his former self.'

'Maybe. But even shadows can loom large. I'm not sure I should risk it.'

'No? Not even for the sake of working with your beloved Tommy again?'

'Oh, that was a low blow — trying to tempt me with that.' Ryan let go a long breath. 'No, no. Tommy's not mine any more. The best I could hope for is to be his strapper or something. I don't have a trainer's licence.'

'Not yet. But I'm not without influence although I haven't tested it lately. I might be able to help you do something about that. Don't make up your mind right now. I want you to take your time and think it through before you refuse me. We can be of assistance to each other in this.'

'I'm still not sure.'

'Of course not. Your world has been turned upside down and you don't know where you are. We won't speak of this again until after the funeral.'

★ ★ ★

Joanne's funeral was a simple cremation with no sentimental eulogy and very few flowers. Since she rarely left home, she had no real friends so not many people bothered to attend, even for Ryan's sake. Fiona also stayed behind, promising to meet up with them afterwards at the pub.

Later, as they sat there with unwanted drinks in front of them and lost in their own thoughts, neither Val nor Ryan had much to say. It was left to Fiona to keep the ball of trivial conversation rolling.

'I loathe funerals,' she said, pulling a long face. 'In my opinion, they're a medieval concept and largely out of date. Somebody needs to rethink the whole process.'

'So what would you prefer, Fee?' For once Glen was less than patient with his new love. 'Build a big lime pit like the paupers' graves in the Middle Ages or what?'

'Have a care here.' Val felt bound to break in, having seen Ryan's stricken expression. 'Don't you realize how callous that sounds?'

'Yeah. Sorry,' Glen said, having the grace to look shamefaced.

'Everyone's suffered because of the cyclone,' Fiona said, patting her overworked hair. Ryan gave a wan smile, thinking she had suffered little damage to her own trivial lifestyle. 'And what are you smirking at?'

Ryan shrugged. Really, he was beginning to think his best option might be to go back to Melbourne with Val. Anything would be better than living here with Mike's father and Fiona, who had taken to watching Tinka like a hawk, waiting for her to make a mistake so that she could be banished from the house.

There was no sign of the little dog when they returned to the Harrison home and she didn't respond to Ryan's call. Usually, she would come running to the door to meet him after any absence. He was, after all, her last link to Joanne.

'Tinka? Tinkie, where are you?' he called, fearing that the little dog might have run off and got lost.

'You don't need to yell — she's outside,' Fiona said through pursed lips. 'I had to put her out in the kennel. She soiled my new white rug — completely ruined it in fact — '

Recalling the dilapidated kennel that once housed a much larger dog and was probably full of lice or fleas, Ryan took off towards it, calling her again. She didn't respond.

Inside the kennel, he found the little dog

shivering and whimpering, attached to a chain that was much too large for her, dragging on her little collar. One eye was closed and she flinched when he touched her back. It was obvious that she had been strapped.

Val was next to arrive behind him.

'Oh no,' she whispered. 'The poor little thing has been beaten. How could anyone be so cruel?'

After releasing Tinka from the heavy chain, Ryan placed the trembling animal in Val's comforting arms and straightened his shoulders to confront Glen and Fiona, who were making their way towards them, taking their time.

Fiona was staring at the ground, refusing to meet his gaze.

'OK, so I lost my temper,' she muttered. 'But it was a new rug — '

Ryan didn't hesitate. As soon as she drew close enough, he gave her an open-handed slap across the face with the full force of his strength behind it.

Her legs gave way and she sat down, looking astonished as much as hurt, blood starting to ooze from where she had bitten her lip. Gingerly, she put her hand to her mouth and started to weep when her fingers came away covered in blood.

Glen's reaction was equally impulsive. He punched Ryan to the ground with two quick blows and stood over him, ready to administer more punishment. All this happening in the space of less than a minute.

'Stop!' Val grabbed Glen by the arm, trying to stand between them. 'Stop it, both of you, before someone ends up in hospital.'

Glen shook Val off but she had succeeded in making him stand away from Ryan. After hauling the weeping Fiona to her feet, he put a supportive arm around her, half-lifting, half-dragging the woman back to the house. Ryan scrambled to his feet, feeling his jaw to make sure it wasn't broken, watching them go. Val was the first to speak.

'I can't believe you did that.' She gave a nervous laugh. 'You seemed to me such a stoic, even-tempered person.'

'Except when it comes to cruelty to animals — that always makes me see red.'

'Well, Ryan, I'd say that tears it. You've no other choice but to come down to Melbourne with me. Now. Today. We're both done here. You can't go back into that house and I can't accept any more of that woman's grudging hospitality. You wait outside here with the dog while I get our things and ring for a taxi to take us to the airport. Hopefully, we can get tickets and take the dog on the same flight.'

'Val, I'm so sorry. But seeing Tinka like that. It made me so angry that I didn't think.'

'Don't apologize. I understand. That little dog is your only link with the past. I'm sure I'd have done the same in your place. I hope you broke her false teeth.'

'False teeth? I didn't know she had them.'

'Oh, yes. Those choppers are far too shiny and white for a woman of her age.' Val winced, examining the little dog's wounds, although Tinka seemed to be rallying now that Fiona was no longer around. 'And I'll raid their first-aid box for something to put on her eye. These little animals are so sensitive and thin-skinned.'

'Tinka must have been seriously frightened. She isn't usually dirty in the house.'

Val handed the little dog back and she snuggled into Ryan's arms and sighed, hiding her face in his armpit. 'I'll ring for the taxi first and be as quick as I can. The sooner we get to the airport and throw ourselves on their mercy, the better.'

'Can you bring a bottle of water when you come back? I'm dry as a bone and I'm sure Tinka's thirsty after having such a fright.'

'Trust me. I don't want to spend any more time with these people than you do.'

'You don't think we should take her to a vet?'

'There are no bones broken and I think she's more frightened than hurt. We'll take her to our own vet to make sure when we get home.'

# 7

In spite of Val's best efforts, it wasn't possible to get them all on a plane until the early morning of the following day. They spent an uncomfortable night in a cheap motel near the airport, having smuggled the little dog into their room. Tinka, still shivering and not quite over her ordeal, was too timid in these strange surroundings to bark and give herself away. In the early morning, after delivering Tinka to the care of those who would supervise her flight, Val made a phone call to her daughter before they boarded the plane.

'Yes, I know,' she said, growing impatient with Chrissie's seemingly endless queries. 'I'm coming home a lot earlier than you expected but I'll tell you all about it when I get back. It hasn't been the easiest of times. And yes, I made Ryan see sense and he's coming with me — it's quite a long story. Luggage? No. The poor kid's lost nearly everything so you won't need to come in the van. How's Dad by the way? Driving Nurse up the wall, I suppose?'

It was obvious that Chrissie had some choice words on the subject as Val's laugh in response had a bitter edge to it.

'I'm not surprised she left if that's what he called her,' she said. 'That's three nurses he's gone through in almost as many weeks. And no,' she added, 'you're not a lousy cook at all — you just have a limited range. Tell him he can eat what he's given, or transfer to a nursing home. See how he likes the grey meat and overdone cabbage they'll serve up to him there.' She listened again and laughed more sincerely this time. 'Don't worry. Give him one of those heavy-duty pills and I'll hire a new nurse to sort him out when I get back. I'll find a gorgon this time who can give him as good as she gets.' She listened for a few moments before going on. 'Chrissie, it's a long drive and will take you the best part of two hours even on the tollways. I'll drive home if you're tired. Oh, and there's one more thing — we're bringing Joanne's little dog, an Italian greyhound. The poor little thing will be beside herself — she's already missing Joanne and has had an unfortunate experience even before she can get on the plane. I don't know how she'll be when we get her back. We'll wait for you outside Departures, then you can pick us up without paying to park. I think we have to pick the dog up somewhere else. Thanks, darlin' — love you too. See you soon.'

110

*　*　*

Although they drove only across the top of town and Ryan didn't see much of the city, it didn't take him long to decide that Melbourne wasn't at all as he had imagined it to be. He thought the city would be just a larger version of Cairns, but he could see at once that this was a modern, if compact, metropolis, confident and comfortable with its position in the twenty-first century. Brick walls, solid fences and thick hedges marked property lines in the suburbs, creating a privacy unknown in the North where rather ugly mesh fences or open front gardens separated most homes. Here too, there were proper pavements or footpaths for people to get around on foot. His first impression of Melbourne was good and he looked forward to getting to know it better. Although it was not his intention to stay long at his uncle's home, he was now in the very heartland of horse racing in Australia. And he was good at his job. Surely, someone would be willing to take him on? Much would depend on how Tommy received him; if the horse still loved him, it would be almost impossible to leave. But if Tommy was happy here and doing well enough without him, then Ryan would feel free to move on.

From time to time, he glanced at his cousin, Chrissie, who didn't have much to say for herself. His first impression was of a slimmer, younger version of her mother; it was a relief to see nothing of Robert in her. Robert! Even the thought of running into that man again made him shudder, in spite of Val's reassurances that his uncle was embarrassed by his predicament and spent most of his time upstairs in his room, even taking his meals there. It didn't take Ryan long to gain the impression that there was no love lost between Chrissie and her father. It wouldn't be fair to say that she welcomed his setback, but his condition did seem to make life easier for herself and her mother. While Val thought it prudent to let Robert think he was still in charge of the stables, it was clear that in her own quiet way, she had taken over the reins of the business entirely. At Ryan's insistence, she put him to work in the stables right away.

His reunion with Tommy had even the most unsentimental of stable hands blowing their noses. The horse heard his approach and started whinnying with pleasure, even before he caught sight of his old friend. Ryan went into the stall and embraced the animal, hiding his face in his mane as he breathed in the familiar scent of the young horse.

'Oh,' Ryan said at last as Tommy nuzzled

his pockets. 'And I didn't even bring you a carrot.'

One of the lads stepped forward at once and remedied this deficiency. Ryan gave it to him and watched as the horse munched it greedily.

'I'll be damned.' Jim Wolfe, the stable foreman had been watching the reunion. 'That's the first time I've seen him eat anything with enthusiasm since he got here. You'd better take over as his strapper, Mr Lanigan. The sooner the better for everyone, I'd say.'

'Ryan, please. And I'd love to look after Tommy. Just try and stop me.'

★　★　★

He had been in Melbourne for a full week before he ran into Robert at all and this was not in the house but in the stables. He heard his uncle's voice raised in criticism and barking orders, even before he caught sight of him in his wheelchair. He paused in the middle of grooming Tommy, wondering whether to stay out of sight or get it over with at once, revealing himself right away.

'Jim! Get Sam or someone to shift that pile of dung at once.' Robert's voice wasn't as strong as before but still had authority. 'You know I won't tolerate the stink of shit in the stables — '

'Sorry, Mr Lanigan. Won't let it happen again.'

'Better not. And why didn't anyone tell me there was a new boy looking after Tommy? You should have checked with me first.'

'But he's good with the horse, Mr Lanigan — you know how difficult Tommy was. An' Mrs Lanigan said it would be OK.'

'Oh, did she? Well, I'll be the judge of that. Jus' remember I'm still in charge here — not Mrs Lanigan.'

'Right you are, sir.'

Robert put on a falsetto, mimicking him. ' "Three bags full, sir!' Don't you have a mind of your own, Jim? Or have you been told to humour me?'

Jim shrugged, looking uncomfortable.

'Come on, then. Show me my horse. How's he doing? I haven't seen much of him since he came down from Queensland and that idiot truckie drove into me.'

Ryan saw no point in trying to avoid his uncle — he would have to meet up with him sooner or later. Quickly, he slipped a leading rein on Tommy, opened the stable door and marched the horse out. To begin with, Robert had eyes only for his horse.

'My word — you're turning into a beauty,

aren't you? A far cry from the half-starved colt I brought down from the North — '

'That's a lie.' Ryan was so angry, he spoke impulsively before he could think better of it. 'My father gave Tommy the best of everything. He even built a new stable for him.'

'You!' Robert turned his chair to look up at him, finally recognizing the nephew he hoped to have left behind in North Queensland, never to be seen again. 'What in the name of Hades are you doing here?'

\* \* \*

'Well now, Miss Lanigan — Christine.' Colin Walker spread his hands on either side of her personnel file that, to her eyes, looked thin and pitifully small. 'Best not waste time beating about the bush — no point in prolonging the agony. We — that is, the directors and I — have decided to let you go.'

Chrissie felt suddenly numb and felt as if she were hearing Mr Walker from a long way off, although this news was no more than she was expecting. 'I see. Because I'm the newest recruit, I suppose?'

Colin Walker sat back, regarding her. 'That does come into it, of course. But I'm afraid you haven't lived up to your promise and our expectations. We are disappointed in you.'

Chrissie was shocked. 'Disappointed? But why? This is the first I've heard of it. And, apart from time off that was due to me after working through several weekends, I haven't taken any sick leave or — '

'So clearly, you are a clock-watcher. If you were really committed to your job here, you wouldn't be counting the extra hours.'

'I didn't. I don't. I admit I have been distracted with family problems lately. My father had a serious accident and I — '

'Spare me the details — they are of no interest to us here.'

Chrissie closed her mouth, shocked by the man's callousness.

'Also, when you came to us, you never said you were planning a wedding. When we hired you — ahead of many equally promising girls — you never mentioned your intention to marry and take an extended trip overseas — '

'No. It was only to be a holiday — a few weeks. But even that isn't happening now. My fiancé called it off.'

'So? He found you as unreliable as we do, I suppose?'

'Now that isn't fair.' Tears sprang to Chrissie's eyes and her temper rose at the unjust accusation. 'I've always done more than my share of the work here. I've come in early most days. I worked like a dog for you.'

'But I don't need a dog, Christine, I need a reliable law clerk — '

'And my name isn't Christine actually — it's Christalynne.' She took pleasure in correcting him but she could have saved her breath as Walker ignored it.

'I need a young person dedicated to being here. Someone prepared to grow with the company — to be here for the next ten years or more — '

'That's insane. No one can promise you that.'

'Clearly, you can't. Which only goes to show what a mistake we made in hiring you. Clear your desk, Miss Lanigan. You can expect to be paid until the end of the current month.'

'But that's only a week away. And what about holiday pay? Surely I'll be entitled to something for that?'

Walker pulled a face, shaking his head. 'Not here long enough,' he said. 'Sorry.'

'A reference, then?' She had a sinking feeling in the pit of her stomach, already knowing what the answer would be. Sure enough, Walker shook his head yet again.

'Company policy. We don't give out references for people who've been here for less than twelve months. In any case, I don't think you'd like what we had to say.'

'Damn you, then.' Suddenly, Chrissie's temper got the better of her. 'You haven't heard the last of this. Mr Walker. You know of Sir Henry Wheeler, I suppose?'

'Sir Henry? Oh, indeed. A rather colourful character, I'd say.'

'Well, Sir Henry is my mother's uncle. He'll be happy to cause a stir over this. I could even take you to tribunal.'

Colin Walker sat back, smiling thinly through bloodless lips, and somehow she knew this wasn't the first time he'd done this. It was familiar territory to him and he almost enjoyed it, wanting people to cringe and plead. 'That would be most unwise, even with the support of your Mr Wheeler. If word gets around that you're a troublemaker, Miss Lanigan, it may be impossible for you to get hired anywhere. A word here and there. It doesn't take much.'

'You can't do this. You can't stop me from getting employment elsewhere. That just isn't fair.'

'Life is as it is, Miss Lanigan. Nobody promised it had to be fair.'

★　★　★

'How long?' Robert had returned from the stables and was confronting his wife in the kitchen. 'How long has that interloper been living here? Eating at our table. Taking over the care of my best horse.'

Val regarded the angry man, hands on hips, trying not to feel pleased that she could loom over him as he sat in the wheelchair. 'Rob, you need to calm down. You'll have another stroke or something.'

'Oh, you'd like that, wouldn't you? I expect you wish I'd died in that accident. Much tidier than having a cripple to care for. Well, I'm here to tell you I'm not finished yet.' Angrily, he smote the arms of his wheelchair. 'I won't be in this damned chair forever. Then you and Chrissie had better watch out.'

Val stared at him. She knew something that Robert did not; his doctors had told her in no uncertain terms that the nerves in his spine had been severed and he'd never walk again. At the same time, they had warned her to keep that news to herself; he shouldn't be allowed to live without hope of recovery or he might fall into a depression.

'I don't even know why you were there.' Val sighed in exasperation. 'You could have bypassed Sydney altogether. What were you thinking? Driving through the city on unfamiliar roads when you'd already been travelling for hours.'

'If you must know, I was looking for a

decent meal. Something other than the usual cholesterol cocktail from a roadside café.'

'And as usual, you've strayed from the subject. We were discussing Ryan. Instead of complaining, you should be grateful he's here. Hunter's Moon was going into a decline, missing the warmer weather as well as the handlers he's used to. Ryan has given him a new lease of life. He'll be ready to race again soon. Perhaps you'll like to go and see him when he does.'

'And maybe I won't. You haven't heard the last of this, Val. That boy doesn't belong here. He has to go.'

'For God's sake, Rob! He's your brother's child — Joanne's child. Remember you loved her once?'

'That was a long time ago. You'd have a shock if you'd seen her.' Robert's mouth twisted in a sneer. 'An ageing beauty, half her mind gone as well.'

'All the more reason to offer a safe haven to her son. You won't even have to see him, if you don't want to.'

'I don't care. I don't want him here.'

'Why? I suppose he reminds you of the shabby way you treated his father. Paying him a pittance for his share of the stables.'

'He was happy enough at the time. He's the one who wanted to leave.'

'Yes. Because you made life unbearable for him. And now you want to take out your spite on his son. The lad has lost everything — father, mother and home in a matter of weeks. And now you want to part him from the horse that he loves.'

'Sentimental twaddle. It doesn't pay to get too fond of a horse. It's only good for as long as it can race and then it's dog food,' Robert growled, turning his chair towards the door. 'I'm going up to my room. See that I'm not disturbed.'

He steered his wheelchair out into the hall and sped towards the newly installed lift. It had cost a fortune and — in his opinion — made the house look like a cheap hotel, but at least it meant that he could go and come as he pleased on all levels and even out to the stables if he wished. Not that he had been going there much at all lately. But all that must change. It made his stomach twist with jealousy to see Ryan working so contentedly with Hunter's Moon, cementing a bond with the horse he had worked so hard to reclaim.

Upstairs in his study, he gave full rein to the temper building inside him and threw his old-fashioned brass desk set at the wall. Fortunately, the ink had long since dried in the wells but it landed on the floor with a satisfying crash. He waited to see if Val had heard and would come to investigate but there was no sound from below or clatter of footsteps on the stairs.

Women! For the first time in his life his decisions and wishes were being overruled by a whole bunch of them; his wife, his daughter and the females they hired to nurse him. At least he'd had a bit of fun there — intimidating those silly girls.

But he had made some progress; he didn't need a nurse any more. And now it was time to take his life back. His power. He was still in his prime, after all, and if he could no longer order the world as he used to do, he might as well give up and die.

What enraged him more than anything was this latest ploy. Without consulting him, they had brought Ryan, that upstart insolent Queenslander, to live not just in Melbourne but right here in his own home. Then, adding insult to injury, they allowed him to take charge of Hunter's Moon — the horse he had taken so many risks to possess. Here in his very own stables, right under his nose. It made him angry to the point of feeling sick.

Then the solution came to him like a bolt from the blue. Why hadn't he thought of it before? He wasn't helpless or impotent — not at all. There was still something he could do.

After all, the plan had worked once — why not again? He had been passive and acquiescent long enough. It was high time he took up the reins and made people sit up and listen; he was no longer prepared to take a back seat and let womenfolk order his life. No, sir!

Although Val was a doormat these days, he had been fond of her once, especially when he believed she might give him a son. But she was long past her best now and putting on weight. She was all too predictable and he was bored with her. Yes, Robert. No, Robert. Whatever you say, Robert — always trying to please him. When he looked at her now, he felt only mild irritation.

He smiled, recalling how he'd made her pay for her little adventure, over and over again. He could scarcely believe that Val, who had always seemed so timid and thoroughly under his thumb, had actually found the courage to have an affair. It made him wonder about Chrissie, who had appeared so quickly after their wedding. He saw nothing of himself in the girl — she was all Valerie with that dark hair and big, brown Welsh eyes. And there had never been any love lost between them — she despised him and, in turn, he had always made it plain that he would have preferred a son. He'd spent little time with her when she was small and she'd never been a Daddy's girl. But of course she had to be his; vanity wouldn't let him travel too far down any other path. He sighed, thinking it a pity the girl's marriage had fallen through. She was a bad influence on her mother and he'd been looking forward to having her gone from his life.

He glanced around his study, thinking he hadn't spent much time there lately. That must be remedied: he would take charge of his life again, making his presence felt; he'd been an invalid long enough. It was obvious that the room was cleaned regularly and was a lot tidier than he remembered leaving it; his usual pile of papers stacked neatly in the in tray rather than strewn about the desk. His heart lurched as he thought of his private filing cabinet, hoping it hadn't been tampered with, and was relieved to find it still locked and untouched. The keys looked untouched as well, still lying in a small pile of dust inside a Chinese vase that he had told everyone was so valuable and so rare, it must never be handled.

Yes, it was high time he made something happen; something that would make them all sit up and realize he was back. So what if he was short-tempered and sometimes had lapses of memory; he could get past all that.

He unlocked the cabinet and looked for the old diary where he kept his most important numbers — those of minor politicians who owed him a favour, shady bookmakers and that guy — oh, what was his name? Harry — that was it. Just Harry. He'd never been told anything else. The guy had made a brief appearance when the job was done, collected his money in cash and then disappeared like a will-o-the-wisp. And now, if it seemed that the job was only half done, Robert had no one to blame but himself. He'd overlooked Ryan, dismissing him as a child. Unfortunately, at twenty, he seemed very much a man. If Robert had understood this at the outset, the matter could have been dealt with at the time.

He scrabbled through the diary with mounting anxiety, unable to find the number he sought. He couldn't go back to his original contact — the man had been arrested recently, suspected of being involved in the death of a bookie. Robert had no intention of being caught up in all that.

Just as he was about to give up the search, he found it — scribbled on a small piece of paper in tiny writing, tucked into the back of the book. He could only hope the guy hadn't ditched the number — he'd never be able to find him then. He pressed the keys on his mobile and listened. The landline would have been more secure but there was always the possibility that Val or Chrissie might pick up an extension and listen in.

The number rang out healthily and Robert smiled. Still connected, then. He let it ring for some time, hoping it wouldn't go to voicemail but it was answered before that happened. The guy sounded irritated.

'Yes, Robert, what do you want? You were to destroy any record of this number soon as the job was completed. I thought you understood that?'

'Yeah, Harry, but I kept it safe. Nobody knows that I have it.'

'I know.'

'But I need your help one more time. Another little job.'

'No! And no again!'

Robert winced and held the phone away from his ear. The man was shouting now.

'I have a strict rule never to do more than one job for a client. Too dangerous for both of us. We shouldn't even be talking now.'

'But you don't understand. I had an accident.'

'Spare me your troubles. I don't have time for them. I'm going off the air now and you're not to call me again. You'll regret it if you do.'

'But, Harry.' He was pleading now. 'It's me

— Robert. I was hoping you'd treat me as a special case.'

'All my cases are special. And strictly one-off. Safer for everyone.'

'But — you could say this was part of the original job. A loose end.'

'No. I don't leave loose ends. Your job was cleanly executed and paid for. We have nothing further to say to each other.' Harry paused before speaking slowly to emphasize his words. 'And let's be clear on this — make any attempt to contact me on this number again and I'll have to kill you.'

And the call ended abruptly. Robert shivered, suddenly chilled. If most people make such remarks, it can be taken as a joke. But Harry was a professional killer; such a threat had to be taken seriously. Robert threw his mobile down on the desk as if he feared it might bite him.

* * *

'What is it, 'Arry?' The pretty French girl pouted and sat beside him on the sun lounger. 'You were so 'appy a moment ago an' now it's as if the sun 'as gone be'ind a cloud. You are angry?'

'I have a lot to think about, that's all,' he said, pulling her into his lap and feeling inside

127

her bikini to caress her sex, not caring who might be watching. Her body was warm, smelling of sun lotion and the sea as she writhed against his fingers, almost purring like a cat. Ondine, as she liked to call herself, was an expensive luxury, as was this resort, and Harry was running out of cash. He had checked his accounts this morning and had been shocked by how much he had spent. The job in North Queensland had gone smoothly enough, with no suggestion of foul play and, with the cyclone following it, diverting everyone's interest, the case was unlikely to be reopened or investigated again. He had nothing in the pipeline right now and who was likely to link a job in Melbourne with what happened in far North Queensland? Perhaps he had been too hasty in blowing Robert off.

'Sorry, darl,' he whispered in Ondine's ear. 'Might have to leave for a while. Need to go to Melbourne to clean up some business.'

'I come with you.' She smiled brightly. 'I love Melbourne. It 'as the best shops.'

'No, you won't.' He pinched her bottom hard, making her squeak.

Keeping Ondine was expensive enough without letting her loose around the shops. 'You'll be a good girl and wait for me here.'

'Maybe I don' like to wait.' She pouted,

giving a Gallic shrug. 'Maybe I get new boyfriend.'

'Then I get new girlfriend. Suit yourself.' Without any warning he tipped her off, letting her fall awkwardly onto the sands. 'See you later, girl. Hop it now. I need to make some phone calls.'

# 8

Having made up his mind to take back the mantle of power, Robert lost no time in giving orders and throwing his weight about in the stables. He found Jim Wolfe and Val looking at Tommy in his stall and making plans. Inwardly, he bristled. He'd teach them to try and exclude him; they needed to recognize that Rob Lanigan was back — he'd show them who was in charge.

Aware of the boss's scarcely concealed resentment, Jim Wolfe brought him up to speed, informing him that now Hunter's Moon was settled in Melbourne, he was to start racing again. Lightly, at this time of year, in the hope of securing him a place in some of the races leading up to the Spring Carnival. Jim and Val intended him to start slowly, allowing him to prove himself in the country before bringing him up to one of the major racecourses in town. Robert was quick to override this decision.

'Tommy doesn't need to waste time doing that. He's a city runner who's already won major races in Sydney. Why waste his energy by letting him race in the country? No. We'll have him racing at Flemington at the end of the month.'

Jim and Val exchanged worried glances but it was Val who spoke. 'Tommy's new to Melbourne and unused to racing here. Besides, he's been living quietly for some time. Put him in front of a city crowd and he might get spooked.'

'Nonsense. It isn't as if he's an untried colt — he's a champion. Cancel the entry for the local meeting. Who did you have down to ride him, anyway?'

'Mac Wesley.'

Robert almost snorted in disgust. 'Wesley? That burnt-out old has-been? He'll take Tommy round as though it's a walk in the park. No. I want somebody hungry — someone with fire in the belly.'

'Tommy doesn't respond well to rough handling,' Val said, grateful that Ryan had made himself scarce and wasn't around to hear Robert's words. 'Who would you suggest?'

'Someone up and coming — young but not too young. A talented rider — Fancy Patterson maybe. She's tough enough and I can overlook the fact that she is a girl.'

'That's debatable.' Jim gave a wry smile. 'Some people say she's more man than most of the boys.'

'Like I said — doesn't worry me.'

Jim's smile faded. 'Rob, with all due respect, you've been out of touch for some time. Fancy Patterson has a bit of a reputation — '

'Yes. For bringing in city winners.'

'And she's been suspended more than once for careless riding and unnecessary use of the whip.'

'So what? All jockeys get suspended from time to time.' He glared at them. 'What's wrong with everyone, all of a sudden? The racing industry used to be about men with some backbone. These days it seems to be run by a bunch of old women.' He cast a disparaging look at Val.

'It's not just about winning, Rob.' Val was seething inside that he should dismiss her in front of Jim, but she kept her voice reasonable and low. 'It's about getting round safely; making sure everyone arrives back at the winning post in one piece.'

'What are you talking about? It's a sport, you numbskull. There has to be some element of risk, some excitement. You'd play it like women's afternoon tennis.'

'All right, I'll meet you halfway,' she said. 'We'll race Tommy at Flemington if that's what you want but we're sticking with Mac, who's already worked with the horse. I don't want to hire Fancy Patterson.'

'OK. OK. Whatever you say.' Robert closed his eyes in exasperation.

He wasn't about to tell her that he'd already arranged for Hunter's Moon to compete in a listed race and that Fancy Patterson had agreed to take the ride.

Val didn't find this out until they were all there at the track, watching Ryan parade the horse. Chrissie was there, too, wearing a sharp black suit she had expected to wear for court appearances but that wasn't going to happen now. She had also treated herself to a cute hat in hot pink and black; it perched on the back of her head and somehow brought out the beauty of her eyes. Covertly, Ryan watched her with admiration, feeling drawn to her until an unwelcome thought popped into his head. His friend Mike would make short work of Chrissie if he saw her looking so sharply dressed, although he wouldn't give her a second glance in the old T-shirts and denims she usually wore at home. Ryan had been in touch several times to tell Mike he was living in Cranbourne although he was in no hurry to tell his friend why he had left Canesville so precipitately. Glen would fill him in on the details soon enough and Mike would have to decide whose side he was on. So far, Mike had been too busy with work and study to drive out to Cranbourne and

Ryan was no longer so keen to see him; not on his uncle's property, anyway. He decided that if Mike could overlook what had happened in Queensland and was genuine about wanting to keep up a friendship, he'd meet him in Melbourne, avoiding the risk of his meeting Chrissie. Talk around the stables was that she had one broken romance behind her already. She didn't need to get mixed up with a woman-chaser like Mike, who was bad news for any girl.

But he set these disquieting thoughts aside as the jockeys arrived on course, ready to take their rides, and he looked around for Mac Wesley, unable to spot him. Where was he? Surely, the old guy hadn't forgotten? He'd been looking forward to taking this ride. Instead, he saw a sharp-featured little woman walking purposefully towards his horse.

'Excuse me,' Ryan said as the woman grabbed Tommy's reins, preparing to mount. 'We're waiting for Mac Wesley. I think you've made a mistake.'

'You're the one who's made the mistake, sonny.' Without his assistance, Fancy Patterson jumped expertly into the saddle. 'Mr Lanigan booked me for this ride today. The ole fella — Wesley — got put out to grass.'

'What's happening, Ryan?' Val had seen Fancy take the horse and was quick to catch up with them, breathless from running across the mounting yard. 'Where's Mac?'

'I don't know,' Ryan said, still holding on to Tommy, who was clearly ill at ease with this new rider. 'This lady says Mr Lanigan dumped Wesley and booked her instead.'

'Did he, indeed?' Val muttered, casting a narrow-eyed look at her husband, who was sitting high up in the front of the stands in his wheelchair, smiling down at them. Rob gave her a mocking salute and she sighed. 'Nothing I can do about it now.' But she held on to the reins for a moment before allowing Fancy to ride away, speaking clearly to make her point. 'For your own safety, Ms Patterson, I'd advise you to limit the use of your whip. Tommy's good-natured and willing but he's a big, strong boy and won't take kindly to any ill-treatment.'

'Are you trying to teach me my job, Mrs Lanigan?' Fancy jerked the reins out of Val's hands, making Tommy flatten his ears and shake his head. 'A colt needs firm handling — he has to be shown who's the boss.' So saying, she dug in her heels and gave Tommy a sharp slap on the rump, making him leap forward and take off at speed.

Val bit her lip and shook her head, exchanging a glance with Ryan, who folded his arms, watching the erratic progress of horse and rider as they made their way to the starting gate.

'Don't worry.' He tried to reassure Val. 'Tommy won't put up with her nonsense for long. She'll be the one to come off worst.'

'But we need him to win,' Val groaned. 'With Mac at least we might have stood a chance.'

Hunter's Moon wasn't used to being treated with so little respect and went through his range of tricks in the hope of unsettling the girl. It didn't work. In less than five minutes, she had him in his appointed stall, waiting for the start of the race.

If Fancy Patterson had only trusted her mount and been less arrogant, all might have been well. But as soon as the starter gave the order and the field made that first leap from the stalls, Fancy tried to get his attention by giving him a sharp crack of the whip. Infuriated by her ongoing lack of respect, Tommy changed gait and sidestepped, dumping his unwanted cargo on the ground. Then, finally free of his burden, he put his head up and set about the task of winning the race.

For the crowd, the rest of the race was uneventful. When Tommy had passed the post ahead of the field, dismissed as 'that unruly horse from Queensland', the race was won by the short-priced favourite. Ryan quickly caught up with his charge, who was being restrained by the Clerk of the Course.

'You're a very naughty boy,' Ryan said, rubbing the horse's nose and giving the lie to his words as he tried not to laugh. Tommy flicked his ears at him and tossed his head in a 'don't care' gesture.

Fancy Patterson was bruised from landing on her bottom on the hard ground but, once she had decided she was unhurt, she was vociferous in her complaints. 'Rob Lanigan told me that horse was a champion,' she raged at Val. Wisely, Robert had not come down from his perch in the stands. 'He shouldn't be on a racetrack at all. He's barely trained. And you can tell Mr Lanigan not to call me again. Mac Wesley can have his ride back and good luck to him.' Having said her piece, she left them, bruised and limping, showing her temper by whacking her whip against her boot. Watching her leave, Ryan laughed.

'It's not funny, Ryan,' Val said. 'I've known Robert to sell a horse on for doing a lot less.'

Ryan sobered immediately but it wasn't just Val's words that were wiping the smile from his face. He had caught sight of Chrissie in the members' enclosure, accosted by a good-looking guy who was attempting to have a serious conversation with her. Unfortunately, he couldn't wait to see the outcome as he had to take Tommy back to the holding stables and rub him down. Val came with him.

'I'll look after Tommy for a while, Ryan. You go and have a drink — have a bit of fun for a change. You never take any time off.'

'Don't you need to get back to Mr Lanigan?'

'Mr Lanigan can look after himself for once. He's done enough damage for one day, hiring that wretched Patterson girl. Poor Tommy.'

'Tommy's all right, he's a tough one. I tried to tell her she'd come off worse.'

'And a wasted race. All because Rob wouldn't take my advice.' Val sighed. 'Go on. Come back in half an hour or so and we'll pack Tommy into the float and take him home.'

'You weren't serious when you said Mr Lanigan might sell him?'

'No, no.' Val was quick with her reassurance, sounding more confident than she felt. 'He has too much invested in him.'

★ ★ ★

'What are you doing here, Tony? How did you get in?' Chrissie's heart was beating wildly, feeling as if it would burst right out of her

138

chest. Until this moment she had thought herself cured of her passion for her erstwhile fiancé but his sudden reappearance in her life was unnerving her. She couldn't help but remember the familiarity of his face as it used to loom over her when they were lying naked in her bed. She recalled his solemn expression and the sleepy, helpless look of lust in his eyes that she had mistaken for love. Hastily, she returned to the present, forcing these visions from her mind. 'This part of the course is reserved for owners and trainers. You have no business coming here.'

'I know that.' He waved her objections away. 'But I needed to see you. I still have that card you gave me.' He shrugged, venturing the mischievous smile that had always undone her before. 'So I held on to it, thinking it might be useful some day and it was.'

'Well, you can give it back to me now. And then you can leave,' she said, refusing to meet his gaze and hoping he wouldn't see how his sudden appearance upset her.

'Aw, Chrissie, don't be like that. Not after all we were to each other.'

'Until you met that blonde you liked better.'

'Oh, she's long gone. I can scarcely remember her name.' Tony waved his hand as if batting away a fly. 'But I needed to see you,

Chrissie. To tell you what a terrible mistake I'd made.'

'No, Tony, you did the right thing for both of us. You were honest, for once. Until then, I never realized you thought of me as no more than an unpaid servant; the idiot who did all your work for you when we were at college — a convenient doormat.'

'No, no. I never thought of you in that way. I've always loved you and I know you loved me.' He put his head on one side, assessing her. 'And you're looking fabulous today. Love the hat. Lost some weight, as well, haven't you?'

'No business of yours if I have.'

'Oh, Chrissie, I put you through hell, didn't I? I'm so sorry.'

'Easy for you to say now.'

'No, it's not easy at all. I have to live with myself. Chrissie, why don't you answer my calls? I need to talk to you — to explain what happened to me.'

'You just don't get it, do you, Tony? I don't pick up because I have nothing to say to you. I just don't care any more.'

'I don't believe you. Love doesn't die that easily.'

'Yes, it does. If it's poisoned by betrayal.'

'Please, Chrissie. I've been a complete ass — I admit it freely — but even a fool deserves a second chance. I need you to forgive me, Chrissie.'

'Tony, you were my first love; you will always be special for that reason alone. We had our time together and I'll never forget it. Fool that I was, I adored you. But I can't take you back. I won't put my life in the hands of a man I can't trust. It would be like trying to build a house on quicksands.'

'You can't mean this. I'm devastated. Please let me hope that one day you'll come around?'

'Tony, listen and believe me. It's over between us.' Slowly, she shook her head. 'And I won't reconsider. This time it's for good.'

'Oh. Well . . . ' He took a deep breath and looked over her shoulder into the distance as if searching for something to say; what new argument he could use to persuade her. He dropped his voice and moved in closer so that she would be the only person to hear what he had to say. 'I had to see you cos I'm in a bit of jam. I've no one else to turn to or I wouldn't ask. But . . . I know you always bring a few hundred to the races, for a meal perhaps or to have a bit of a punt. Don't suppose you could see your way clear to lending me some?'

'So that's it. You want money from me,' Chrissie muttered as her heart gave a painful lurch. This was the same old Tony, going from one crisis to the next, expecting other people to bail him out. He hadn't changed at all. 'How much do you need?'

'Only a couple of hundred.' He scrubbed his hands through his hair, gabbling in his eagerness to make her understand his predicament. 'Three maybe, if you can spare it.' His eyes glittered, sure he had her now; that she would come to his rescue. 'Promise I'll get it back to you soon as I can — ' He stopped in mid-sentence as she took a step away from him, wide-eyed and shaking her head. 'Whassamatter, Chrissie? What?'

'I don't believe this. After all that's happened between us, you have the nerve to come here, asking me to give you money.'

'No, no, not give. Lend.'

'Give. Lend. It makes no difference with you. I'll never see it again. I don't have much money, anyway. You do know I lost my job?'

'Yeah, but your daddy's well off.' He dismissed it with a shrug. 'He wouldn't see you go short.'

'You have no idea, have you?' She closed her eyes briefly to stop herself from screaming. 'Tony, just go. Now. Before I talk to some officials and have you thrown out.' She looked at him, seeing for perhaps the first time what a pathetic opportunist, what a cringing little person he really was. How could she ever have thought she was in love with him? 'And please, do me a favour and stay out of my life.'

'Right.' He dropped the mask at last, narrowing his eyes in spite. 'I can see how much I was mistaken in you. I've had a lucky escape.' Determined to have the last word, he tore the card she had given him into tiny pieces and scattered them. 'All that time we were together and I never knew what a bitch you can be. You don't even care that I could be beaten up and left for dead in some alley.' And, head high, he strode away from her.

'It won't be my fault if you are,' she called after him, equally determined to have the last word, and watched his angry, retreating back until it disappeared from view. Out of the corner of her eye, she saw someone taking multiple photos of him with a mobile phone but thought nothing of it at the time. Whatever trouble Tony had brought on himself, it was no longer her affair. It was only when she was quite sure he was gone that she gave way to gasping sobs and the tears came.

Ryan, who had been watching them discreetly from a distance, waited until he was quite sure Tony was gone, before hurrying to her side, shielding her from public view while she regained her composure. He was still wearing his blue strapper's vest with Tommy's race number on it.

'What's happened, Chrissie? What did that bastard say to upset you? I'll catch up with him and thump him into the middle of next week, I'll — '

'Ryan,' she laughed weakly. 'He's not worth it. There's no need for you to play the white knight.' She fished a tissue out of her handbag and blew her nose heartily. 'Really, these are tears of relief because he's finally gone.'

'Then let me buy you a drink to celebrate. Something strong enough to buck you up.'

'I could murder a gin and tonic.'

'Coming up.'

While he was gone, Chrissie blotted her cheeks and applied a little make-up to hide the fact that she had been crying. When he returned with the drinks, she gave him a bright smile and thanked him.

'To you,' he said, quaffing his beer as she took a few quick gulps of her gin and tonic, enjoying the quick buzz of the alcohol on an empty stomach.

'Thank you, Ryan,' she said. 'I needed that.'

'Who was . . . ?' he started to say and then changed his mind. 'No, it isn't my business. You don't have to say anything, if you don't want to.'

'It isn't a secret. He's the man I once expected to marry,' she told him. 'But he turned out not to be the person I thought. I had a lucky escape,' she said, echoing Tony's last words.

'I see.'

'Do you?' She smiled, wondering if he did. 'Ryan, have you ever been in love?'

'No, not really.' He felt awkward with this line of questioning. 'You see, we lived way out in the bush and my mother was — she didn't like people coming to the house. Sometimes I went into town with my best friend, Mike, but he was the one the girls always went for, not me.'

'Then they were idiots,' she said, bringing a sudden blush to his cheeks. What a sweet, old-fashioned, unspoiled young man he was. He had a quiet strength and lots of potential. What a pity he was so much younger than she was.

He's your cousin, you fool! she lectured herself. Quite aside from the fact that he's twenty and you're almost twenty-seven. What was wrong with her? Half a glass of G and T and she was ready to throw herself at Ryan's feet. It must be a reaction from seeing Tony and sending him away for the last time.

Ryan watched the colour suffusing her face and wondered what she was thinking. He was halfway in love with her already; a heady feeling that was also strange to him. If this was love, then it was far from comfortable. But for the first time in his life, he started to understand Mike. Was it any wonder that his friend pursued love with such dedication if this was how it felt? Anticipation was everything. He looked at the imprint of Chrissie's lips on her glass and wondered what it would be like to kiss her. He had no idea that she was feeling just as awkward and thinking the very same thing.

# 9

Robert kept quiet about what happened shortly after the race. He was taking the lift to the ground floor, prior to going home, having steered his wheelchair to the back of the lift. After the embarrassing performance of Hunter's Moon, he felt he was being deliberately ignored. Nobody wanted to talk to him, not even Dickie Yerbook, the tactless presenter from one of the TV stations that most people detested and tried to avoid. The small amount of publicity just wasn't worth putting up with the man's boorish comments and personal remarks, although he himself resembled a sausage bursting out of its skin in his shiny suits. He believed himself to be a great wit and a fine source of knowledge around the track but the truth was that most people didn't like him well enough to share any inside knowledge. So, when it came to tipping, he had to play it safe, advising people to follow the favourite.

Robert hoped that by leaving before the last race he might have the lift to himself but he was wrong. Tired after a long day at the track, a lot of people crowded in after him. In a wheelchair, he was at a disadvantage, having to look up at everyone, and he felt a stab of irritation as people chatted over his head, ignoring him. Then he saw a face he recognized, causing his heart to step up its beat. To be certain, he watched the man covertly as he spoke to his friends and soon recognized his distinctive, gravelly voice. Yes, it was Harry, the ex-military man he had hired to go to North Queensland and who had been so angry at first when he suggested a second commission. Harry and his friends were in a celebratory mood; obviously they had won some money and already spent quite a lot of it on booze.

He had been surprised and a little suspicious when the man returned his call, apologizing for his hasty refusal and eager to meet to discuss the new job. Already Robert was thinking better of hiring him again — the man's attitude had been threatening and it could be asking for trouble to trust him again. But, tempted by the thought of losing the thorn in his side that was Ryan, he quickly overcame any thought of regret. So he arranged to meet Harry in the car park of the hospital where he went for his weekly course of physiotherapy. Val dropped him off there, arranging to pick him up an hour later after his session so he expected to have more than enough time to make his arrangements with Harry before she returned.

Efficient as ever, Harry arrived on time and Robert gave him his instructions as well as a large deposit. The remainder was to follow when the job was done.

'And here are the ground rules,' Robert said. 'I don't want to see you anywhere near my place in Cranbourne — no foul play on my own doorstep.' He knew it sounded rude but he didn't care; after all he was paying the bills. 'We'll all be at Flemington on Saturday for the races, so you can pick up the guy there where it'll be nice and anonymous. You'll know him at once — tall and fair-haired — always making sheep's eyes and hanging around my daughter. That's her,' he said, thrusting a recent photo of Chrissie into Harry's hands.

Harry squinted at it. 'What about the bloke? Got one of him, too?'

Robert didn't answer because out of the corner of his eye he could see Val driving into the car park in the distinctive yellow bubble that had been purchased to carry him in his wheelchair — in a previous life it had been a taxi for the disabled. Silently, he cursed her for coming back early — nine times out of ten he had to wait because she had been shopping and lost track of time.

'You need to leave — my wife's here early and I don't want her to see you,' he muttered. 'You have your instructions, OK? Now go on — get the hell out of here.'

'Hold on — this is all very vague and I need to be clear on this.' Harry frowned, more than a little irritated by Robert's lack of respect. He'd love to snub Robert and refuse the job but he was short of money and desperately needed it. 'How do you want it done this time? Straight-up murder is easy but making it look like an accident will cost you more.'

'I don't care — just get it done. Push the little bastard in front of a bus if you like.'

'Hmm. Don't think so. Messy.' Harry leaned forward and grinned. 'You really don't like the guy, do you? What's he done? Disrespected your precious daughter?'

Robert frowned, ignoring these queries. 'You need to get going. Now. Before my wife sees you.'

'Righto, General. Keep your hair on.' After tucking the photo of Chrissie into his top pocket, Harry moved away just as Val pulled up alongside them.

'Why didn't you wait inside, Rob?' she said as she left the driver's seat to open the hatch and put down the ramp to let him in. 'You'll catch your death out here in this wind.'

'Because I'm fed up with waiting about inside hospitals — the air is stifling and I don't like the smells,' he muttered. 'I'll be glad when I'm back on my legs and can stop all this rehab and physio nonsense. Doesn't seem to do me much good, anyway.'

Val bit her lip, knowing very well that it didn't; if there was any benefit at all it was mental rather than physical. 'And who was that man you were talking to?' she asked, watching Harry drive away. 'I haven't seen him before.'

'No one for you to worry about,' Robert said hastily. 'Just another patient, passing the time of day.'

'Didn't look like a patient to me — too fit to have anything wrong. And the way you were talking — heads close together like that — much too intense for a casual chat. You're up to something, aren't you, Rob?'

'No, I'm not!' he yelled, finally losing it. 'Are we going to stand here all day discussing a stranger or can we go home?'

'Yes, of course. Sorry.' Val helped Robert wheel himself into the back of the car. He said nothing more about Harry, hoping she'd forget all about him. After a while he convinced himself that she had.

So he wasn't expecting to see Harry again and certainly not in the same lift at the races.

Further recognition was not what he wanted at all. He hunkered down in his wheelchair, hoping not to be seen. But just before Harry left the elevator, laughing and cracking jokes with his mates, he turned towards Robert and put two fingers to his eyes and then he grinned, giving a 'thumbs up' sign.

What did that mean? Robert wished he knew. Did he mean the job was done or merely that he had it in his sights? He shivered, suddenly chilled, only now realizing what a chain of events he had set in motion and too late to change. He knew that Harry enjoyed what he did, relishing the violence and priding himself on not leaving any loose ends. Alone and in a wheelchair, Robert felt exposed and vulnerable. Experience had taught him that most people preferred to ignore the disabled and not get involved. Good Samaritans were few and far between. What a simple matter it would be to tip a helpless man out of his wheelchair in the midst of a drunken, jostling crowd. What was to stop Harry killing him once he'd been paid?

The lift reached the ground level and suddenly Val was there at his side — motherly and solicitous. 'Good heavens, Rob, you look awful,' she said. 'You should take one of your pills.'

'Don't fuss, woman. I'm all right,' he growled at her, although he had never been so pleased to see anyone in the whole of his life.

'Done too much today, haven't you?' she said, wheeling him towards the car park. 'No wonder you're such a grouch. Let's get you home.'

★ ★ ★

Later, she was surprised when he backed off, letting her take over the training of Hunter's Moon and reinstating Mac Wesley as Tommy's jockey for both track riding as well as on race days. She was a firm believer in allowing a trusting relationship to develop between rider and horse, rather than take pot luck on what rider may or may not be available on a day. She had been bracing herself for still more opposition from Robert wanting her to hire yet another high-profile jockey, but the experience with Fancy Patterson seemed to have left him subdued and willing to fall in with her plans. And she could feel nothing but relief when no further mention was made of selling the horse.

While Robert rode home with Val, Chrissie was preparing to drive the jeep home with Tommy in the horsebox behind it. Ryan had already put the protective socks on his legs and was loading the horse.

'Will you look at him!' Exasperated, Chrissie was shaking her head. 'Still full of himself. Anyone'd think that he won.'

'He finished first, didn't he? Horses aren't silly, you know. Of course he thinks he won. And he would have done, too, if that silly woman had listened to your mother.'

'Fancy Patterson never listens to anyone,' Chrissie sighed.

'So what happens now?' Ryan climbed into the passenger seat beside her. 'What will your father do?'

'He won't sell him, if that's what you're worried about. The plain fact is that he can't afford to. Mum already spoke to Mac Wesley and he's coming back. She wants him to work with the horse and get him ready for the Spring Carnival.'

'That's good,' Ryan said, unable to hide his relief. 'I'll drive us home, if you like,' he offered. 'You must be tired, after that upset with your ex — '

'I don't want to talk about Tony, thank you.' She held up a hand to stop the flow of his words. 'He's gone from my life and this time it's for good. I don't even want to think about him any more.'

'No, of course not. Sorry.' Ryan felt

miserable; he should know better than to open old wounds.

'No, I'm sorry,' she said, taking off her jacket and hat, laying them across the back seat where they wouldn't get crushed. 'It wasn't your fault and I shouldn't take my temper out on you.'

Ryan looked away, realizing he was in danger of staring at her pretty bosom, tantalizingly revealed in the pale pink silk blouse she was wearing under her suit. He was even more aware of her perfume as well, now she had taken her jacket off. It was something spicy and exotic, setting his senses reeling. He steadied himself by taking a deep breath.

'OK,' he said. 'Let's find something less controversial. We have at least an hour's driving ahead of us. Films — we can talk about films. That's always a safe subject.'

'Is it?' She smiled and started the car, after checking the rear-vision mirror to make sure Tommy was settled. 'So tell me, Ryan, what sort of films do you like? Action adventure, I suppose? Things with robots and futuristic machines. Most boys do.'

'Is that how you see me, then? As a silly boy who can't see past guns and fighting machines?'

'No, of course not. I don't think you're silly

at all. Oh dear,' she said, biting her lip. 'Whatever I say, it comes out all wrong. Why do we always get off on the wrong foot?'

'I don't know.' He smiled, shaking his head. 'You're right, though, I do like fantasy. Get that from my mum, I suppose. I'm a big fan of Peter Jackson's work.'

'*The Lord of the Rings* and now the new Hobbit movies. But I've heard some people are critical, saying the writers haven't stuck to the original.'

'And why should they? Those stories were written ages ago for a much more naive generation. We have different technology now and better special effects so why shouldn't film makers take advantage and use them?'

Chrissie laughed. 'How do we manage it? Arguing like politicians even when we're just talking about films.'

'Because I care about films. To me they're a lot more than frivolous entertainment. I had the start of a great Blu-ray collection once.'

Chrissie nodded. She didn't question him further, knowing the cyclone had probably ruined all his possessions. She recalled meeting him from the plane when he arrived in Melbourne having lost all he held dear and bringing next to nothing but his mother's little dog. Tinka had settled happily into the stables at Cranbourne, transferring her affections to the resident elderly greyhound who had become her hero, protecting her from the half-wild stable cats who hissed and would have attacked her if they'd been allowed.

Leaving the city behind, they travelled in silence for some time, each searching for a topic of conversation mild enough to make no waves.

'Do you want a coffee?' she said, having spotted a McDonald's sign up ahead. 'I should probably have one. That was a stiff drink you bought for me at the races.'

'Oh, I'm so sorry — I never thought,' he said. 'I wouldn't like you to lose your licence. Do you want me to drive now?'

'And let you get into even more trouble on a probationary licence? No.'

He stared at her for a moment before speaking. 'Chrissie — seriously — will you do something for me?'

'Yes, of course. What?'

'Stop reminding me that I'm so much younger than you are.'

'Do I really do that?' She looked taken aback.

'Yeah. All the time. Look, I don't want coffee right now. Just pull off the road for a moment — over there on the left, under those trees.'

'Why? Is something wrong? You do know we'll get eaten alive by mosquitoes at this time of night.'

'Just do it, woman.'

'Ryan, I really don't — ' She broke off, shaking her head. All the same, she did as he asked, cutting the engine after pulling in under the trees.

He was out of his seat belt and crushing her in his arms in a moment, almost biting her lips as he ground them under his own before parting her teeth with his tongue. His experience was limited but nothing and no one had ever tasted so good. Vaguely, he was aware of a murmured objection as he unfastened her seat belt and deepened the kiss but he didn't stop because he couldn't. He'd never realized kissing could be like this. He clasped the fullness of her breast in the silk blouse and camisole underneath it and kept on kissing her until the tension left her and gradually she relaxed into his embrace with a small sigh. Pushing the blouse aside, he left a trail of kisses along her neck, so lost to the moment that he was scarcely aware of leaving a bruise in the form of a love bite on her throat.

It was only as he started to unfasten her blouse that she came to her senses and murmured an order that he would have to obey. 'Ryan, please! Ryan, stop!'

He opened his eyes and stared into hers, bracing himself for a sharp slap in the face. It didn't come.

'Now then,' he asked, breathless but still unwilling to let her go. 'Tell me truthfully. Do I seem like a child to you or not?'

For the moment unable to find her voice, she shook her head. Cautiously, still holding her, he sat up, looking into her face. Her hair was on end, her eyes bright and her lips bruised from his kisses. She seemed bemused, almost in a trance.

'Chrissie — do you not know how beautiful you are?'

'Oh, Ryan, I'm not beautiful at all. That's the one thing Tony never lied about.'

'Then Tony was a fool who took you for granted. Is he the only experience you've ever had?'

'Well, we knew each other forever. It started from school.' She began to answer him before deciding against it. 'Anyway, my experience or lack of it is really none of your business.'

'I could make it my business, though.' He grinned at her, bright-eyed and flushed himself from feelings that were all so new. 'I'd say you're not that much more experienced than I am.'

'Are we comparing notes? That's a dangerous game. If you must know, I did sleep with Tony, yes — although he always complained I was clumsy and not much good at it.'

'Maybe he should have taken a closer look at himself.'

'I don't want to talk about Tony. Not now. Let's talk about you instead. It strikes me, Ryan, that we need to find you a girlfriend.'

'Right. Someone my own age, I suppose?'

'Well, yes.'

'Don't you dare try to pull rank. I was there, remember, and I know you enjoyed our kissing just as much as I did. And no — I don't want you to find me a girlfriend, Chrissie. I want you.'

'But Ryan, can't you see how hopeless it is?' She laughed weakly. 'We are cousins — family, and too closely related. If we'd known each other as children, we'd have grown up together and you wouldn't have feelings for me.'

'You can't know that.'

'And for me this is all too soon. Emotionally, I feel bruised. I've only just come to the end of a bad relationship — I need a bit of breathing space and some peace. I don't want to be in love again. Not right now.'

'And you think I do? I know it's uncomfortable and it hurts. But we can't always choose the ones we love. It just happens, doesn't it? Like a bolt from the blue.'

'Oh no, you're a romantic. That's all I need.' Chrissie sighed. 'You haven't thought this through at all, have you? Can you imagine the look on my father's face if we were to tell him — ' She broke off and her expression changed as something occurred to her, making her wince and close her eyes as if caught by a sudden pain. 'Oh, my God. That's it, isn't it? That's what this is about. You don't love me at all — you're just using me to get back at my dad.'

'No! What are you saying? Chrissie, listen to me. How can you think I'd take cruel advantage of you like that?'

'My, but you're good. You had me going there for a moment. I almost believed in you.' She shook her head, blinking back tears that suddenly threatened. After the way Tony had behaved towards her, her self-esteem had been badly damaged, making it hard for her to trust again. She was slipping away behind her barriers and Ryan couldn't find the right words to reach her.

'Come on,' she said wearily, pushing him away and trying to straighten the creases in her skirt. 'You have to put all thought of me out of your mind. It's the only way for us to get past it.'

'I don't want to get past it, Chrissie. And I'm not sure you do, either.'

'Stop pretending you love me because it's not fair. We have to forget what happened between us just now.'

'Because nothing did happen, Chrissie,' he said in a small voice. 'It was just a few kisses.'

'Yes.' She smiled wearily, wishing she hadn't enjoyed them so much. The memory of his passion and youthful enthusiasm would remain with her for some time. 'Just a few kisses.' She tilted the rear-view mirror to check her dishevelled appearance, realizing there was little to be done about the mark on her throat. Hopefully, her lips would look less bruised by the time they arrived back in Cranbourne.

'I don't want to leave it like this — ' he began.

'We don't have any choice. Fasten your seat belt, Ryan, we're leaving. I don't want to stop for coffee or anything now. I just want to get home.'

On the road again, Ryan tried several times to get through to her but she dismissed his attempts at conversation with a shake of her head, keeping her eyes on the road.

'Chrissie!' he said at last, frustrated by her

lack of response. 'Don't do this to me. It's not my fault your ex was a thoughtless bastard who bruised your ego and hurt you. I am not that man — '

'Ryan, that's enough. I don't need to hear any more. Just accept that I saw through what you were doing. The game is up so you can drop the pretence now.'

'Chrissie, you have to believe me — I'm not playing games. I keep trying to tell you this but you won't hear me.'

By now they had arrived at the stables. Chrissie stopped the car and got out, leaving Ryan to garage the vehicle and deal with the horse as she sprinted for the house. She didn't trust herself to say anything without breaking down.

★　★　★

The evening also got worse for Ryan, too. While he was settling Tommy in his stall, Bill Sansome, the vet, arrived, setting down his bag and rolling up his sleeves.

'What's all this about?' Ryan said. 'I don't think Tommy's due for any more shots.'

'After the way he played up at the track, Mr Lanigan wants him gelded,' Bill said. 'He thinks it'll settle the horse so he'll concentrate on his racing.'

'But you can't!' Ryan stood protectively in front of Tommy. 'He's almost the last of a very special line. When his racing days are done, he should be offered for breeding. That was my father's plan.'

'So he should. I don't like this any better than you do. It's a knee-jerk reaction on Mr Lanigan's part.'

'Can't you tell him so? I know he won't listen to me.'

Bill pulled a face. 'Have you ever tried to tell Rob Lanigan anything?'

'If you agree that it's wrong, then why are you doing it?'

Bill Sansome thought for a moment, folding his arms and looking at Tommy. 'It does seem a shame — he's such a magnificent beast.' He brightened, struck by another thought. 'How often does Robert come down to the stables, these days?'

'Hardly at all. We stay out of each other's way as much as we can.'

'OK. Most likely he'll assume that the job has been done. If he finds out it hasn't, I'll tell him I've been so busy lately that it slipped my mind.'

'Oh, thank you so much. You don't know what this means to me.'

'Don't thank me yet. If Rob thinks I forgot to do this on purpose, he'll sack me and get someone else to finish the job.'

'Then I'll have to make sure he doesn't. I do appreciate what you're doing for us, Bill. I'll buy you a beer sometime.'

'I'll hold you to that,' the young vet laughed. 'I might need it too if Rob gives me the sack.'

# 10

Seeing that her mother was on the telephone, Chrissie ran through the kitchen, hoping to reach the sanctuary of her room and indulge in a good, self-pitying weep. This wasn't to be. Val called out, holding the landline towards her.

'I think you need to take this.'

Chrissie took a deep breath and closed her eyes. 'Mum, if that's Tony, I don't want to speak to him.' She didn't break her stride, continuing her progress towards the stairs.

'It's not Tony. It's Mrs Raymond, his mother. And I think you should speak to her. She sounds really upset.'

'Not my problem if she is,' Chrissie muttered, accepting the phone with bad grace. Lena Raymond was the last person she wanted to tangle with; there had never been any love lost between them. Tony's mother had made it plain that she didn't think Chrissie beautiful or talented enough to be a good match for her son. But then, no girl was ever going to reach her exacting standards.

'Yes, Mrs Raymond?' She made it sound as

if she were answering a business call. 'What can I do for you?'

'Nothing at all. Not now.' The woman's voice was thick with tears. 'Oh, Chrissie, he told me he was coming to see you. Why didn't you help him? You've always done so before.'

Chrissie sighed. 'Mrs Raymond, times have changed and we're not together any more. I'm sure you know Tony left me for another girl.'

'Yes, but that didn't mean anything. It was just a silly fling. He realized his mistake and wanted to come back to you — '

'Well, it was too late. How could I trust him again after that?'

'But didn't you see how desperate he was, to swallow his pride and ask for your help?'

'Yes, of course. But Tony and his problems aren't mine. Not any more.' Somehow it was a relief to say it out loud.

'So it doesn't matter to you that he was singled out and attacked on a public street?'

For a moment Chrissie was stunned into silence. 'Well, of course it matters. When did this happen?'

'Earlier this evening as he was leaving the racecourse.'

'Look, Mrs Raymond, I knew Tony was in trouble over his gambling debts and I'm sorry if he's been hurt. But it's time he learned not to tangle with loan sharks. Such people don't play nice.'

'Oh, that's easy for you to say, Chrissie Lanigan — smug and sitting in judgement on everyone.' The woman was angry now. 'They knocked him down in the street and his head struck the kerb. My boy, my lovely Tony — is dead.'

'Oh no!'

'Human beings are frail. They can die so easily. And this time you have to take a share of the blame. I want you to think about that.' And, choked by a fresh storm of tears, Mrs Raymond left Chrissie with the dial tone. Stunned and struggling to assimilate this latest news, she walked slowly across the room and carefully returned the telephone to its stand.

'What is it?' Val said, having heard only one side of the conversation. 'Has something happened to Tony? You'd better sit down. You've gone white as a sheet.'

'Yes,' Chrissie said, feeling her way to a chair and collapsing into the cushions, hunched and hugging her knees. 'She says Tony's dead. Knocked down in the street. She thinks he was murdered by loan sharks.'

'Rubbish. Loan sharks damage people but they don't usually kill them. Why murder the goose that will keep on laying those golden eggs?'

'I don't know. But Lena wants to lay the blame at my door. She knew Tony was coming to find me and borrow some money — '

'Of all the nerve, after the way he treated you — '

'Stop it, Mom. None of that matters now. Tony's dead,' Chrissie said through trembling lips as a tear splashed onto her cheek.

'God, yes. I'm sorry. I forgot.' Val considered this for a moment. 'All the same, his mother might have put two and two together and made five. She assumes the debt and the death are connected but maybe they're not. You saw Tony at the races and not long afterwards he has a fight in the street and ends up dead. Maybe he was in a bad mood after seeing you, picked a fight with the wrong person and there was an accident. You hear of these things on the news every day.'

'I know. But I can't help thinking it's partly my fault.'

'Well, don't. If you'd given him money, it could have been stolen, anyway.'

'All this is giving me a headache, Mum. I need to go to bed.'

'You haven't had any dinner.'

'I don't want any. I couldn't eat a thing.' Chrissie heaved herself from the chair and started towards the stairs.

'Until we find out what really happened to Tony, I won't have you blaming yourself,' Val called after her.

And with her mind full of this latest drama, Chrissie forgot all about the misunderstanding with Ryan and the heartache it had caused her.

⋆  ⋆  ⋆

Robert was in the stables when his mobile rang. He looked at the caller ID and wasn't pleased to see it was Harry.

'Didn't I tell you not to call me here? We agreed that I'd get back to you with the rest of the money as soon as I knew the job was done — '

'Yes and that was a week ago,' Harry snapped back. 'I'm getting tired of waiting. I have things to do and need to get out of here, pronto!' He was thinking of Ondine, who had probably given up on him by now and found somebody else. He didn't care if she had; but if she was waiting for him, it would save him the trouble of finding another girl.

'Of course I'll pay you, Harry, but not until the job is done. And while you're there, I'd like to know what's taking so long.'

'Are you deaf? I told you — your job was

completed a week ago — outside the racecourse, just like you said.'

'That so? Then why can I hear the lad whistling along to the radio while he's grooming my horse!'

'He — he works for you?' For the first time Harry sounded uncertain. 'You never said that.'

'Didn't I? How much clearer can I be? I told you — the lad who's always hanging around my daughter.'

'You never said there might be more than one. In my business, I need very clear instructions. You told me I'd see this guy with your girl at the races — and there he was — large as life and all over her just like you said. Then they had a bit of a spat and he left. I follow, pick a scrap with him outside in the street and make certain he falls down hard enough to break his head. Then I get out of there fast while everyone's still in shock, looking at him lying in the road, bleeding out. Funny thing, that. People are always fascinated when there's a lot of blood.'

'Spare me the details.'

'Bit late to be squeamish, isn't it?' Harry laughed. 'So there 'tis. An unfortunate accident, all nice and anonymous just like you said. The job is done and now I'd like to be paid.'

'You killed the wrong bloke, you idiot!'

Robert hissed down the phone — glancing around to make sure he wasn't overheard.

'If I have, it's your fault. You were so freaked about your wife turning up early that day, you sent me off without proper instructions — '

'Then you should have checked. You can't go around killing people at random in the street.'

'Is zat so?' Harry was mocking him now. 'It's what I do for a living, remember?'

'Well, I'm not paying for your mistakes,' Robert said, totally rattled and trying to keep the tremor from his voice. 'You can keep the money I've already paid but I'm not — '

'Thanks. I've already spent it.'

'Fine but don't expect any more. Get out of Melbourne and make yourself scarce. I don't want to hear from you ever again.' So saying, Robert cut the call, determined to have the last word although the altercation had left him shaking and shivering like an old man.

'Oh no, Robbie,' Harry repeated softly, tapping his phone against his teeth. 'You should remember who you're dealing with — you don't get to blow me off that easily.' He smiled to himself. He knew more than one way to get money out of a client unwilling to pay.

★  ★  ★

Ryan didn't know what to do. Every time he tried to get through to Chrissie, he came up against a blank wall. In hindsight, he realized that his approach had been clumsy and without finesse; no wonder she believed he had an ulterior motive. But now she would give him no opportunity to convince her of his sincerity. She didn't ignore him completely — other people would wonder why — but she made sure they were never alone and answered his questions with a listless 'yes' or 'no'. She had retreated behind her barriers and there seemed to be no way for him to get through to her.

On the brighter side, Mac Wesley was making good progress with Tommy. Ryan had taken the horse to Caulfield that day and they had won quite a long and difficult race against a fairly large field and he was in high spirits as he returned the horse to his stable. Tired but happy, he thought even Robert would have to be pleased with this latest triumph, although he didn't expect any praise from that quarter. His uncle was sure to point out that it was only a midweek meeting and not even a listed race. All the same, so long as Tommy remained fit and free of injury, he would be an outstanding horse to watch during the Spring Carnival, now only a matter of weeks away.

After making sure Tommy was fed and comfortable in his stall, Ryan made his way back to the house, hungry and looking forward to an early supper. Having spent the day seeing to the horse's needs with no one to help him, he hadn't had time to eat anything much himself.

About to open the kitchen door, he heard Chrissie's distinctive giggle in response to a male voice. It occurred to him they'd heard little of her laughter in the weeks following Tony Raymond's funeral. The body had been quickly released for burial when the coroner brought in a verdict of accidental death during an affray that, according to witnesses, Tony seemed to have started himself. No criminal charges had been brought against anyone and, in spite of Lena Raymond's ongoing complaints, the case appeared to be closed. Everyone, including Chrissie, would have to move on.

But today her infectious giggle was back; in fact she sounded almost flirtatious. Someone was here who'd succeeded in making her laugh. He couldn't help wishing it had been himself.

He opened the door and stopped dead in his tracks when he saw who it was. So much had been happening recently, he had forgotten entirely that Mike Harrison was living in Melbourne. Yet here he was, sitting next to Chrissie, legs crossed and with his feet up on the table, rocking back in his chair and making himself at home in Val's kitchen. They looked quite relaxed and cosy together already, Chrissie with a glass of red wine nearby. She looked flushed and bright-eyed, more animated than he had seen her for some time. There was no sign of meal preparation and Val was nowhere in sight. Ryan took all this in in a matter of seconds, surprised to find that he wasn't more pleased to see his old friend.

'And here he is — the man of the hour!' Mike stood up and came to give Ryan a hug. 'Fresh from victory on the race-course, I hear. How the hell are you, mate?'

'Good. No, I'm great,' Ryan murmured. 'I'd almost forgotten that you were in Melbourne.'

'My fault!' Mike was unusually hearty. 'I should have made the effort and come to see you before.' He turned to Chrissie with a grin that was all mischief. 'And I'd have been here a lot sooner if you'd told me about this lovely cousin of yours.'

Chrissie smiled at the compliment, looking down at her hands in her lap. Oh, Chrissie, not you too! Ryan thought. Can't you see what Mike's doing? Don't be one of his victims, falling for his superficial charm. He had seen girls like this too many times before; staring at Mike with that soft, vulnerable look in their eyes.

'Well, say something!' Mike clapped him on the shoulder. 'Anyone'd think you weren't pleased to see me.'

'Of course I am. It's a surprise, that's all.'

'And so is your gorgeous cousin.' Mike winked. 'I'm looking forward to showing her my favourite places around town.'

'I think Chrissie already knows more places than you do. She used to work in town.'

'Then she can show me hers, too,' Mike said, making sure nobody missed his heavy-handed double meaning.

'Have — er — ' Ryan thought he might as well get the awkward moment out of the way. 'Have you heard from your father lately?'

'Went back home during the last break from college. Wasn't looking forward to it with Fiona ruling the roost — but guess what? Ding, dong, the witch is dead!'

'Fiona's dead?'

'No, silly — nothing quite so dramatic but she's gone, anyway. And from what Pa tells me you had a hand in that.'

'What did he say? We had a bit of a

disagreement — about the way Fiona was handling Mum's little dog. You might as well know, she made me so mad, I lost my temper and knocked her down. Then your father came to her defence and threw a punch at me, too. We left shortly after that. So I'm not sure how he feels about me now.'

'You did him a good turn. Seems that after you left, the argument escalated. Fiona wanted my dad to set the lawyers on you and he wouldn't play. Said you'd suffered enough already and he was sorry he knocked you down as you didn't deserve it. Fiona took off in a huff and went to her sister in Sydney. There, apparently, she remains, waiting for Dad to apologize and reclaim her. Reckon she'll have a long wait.'

'Well, I'm pleased to hear he's out of her clutches and bears no ill will towards me. I always liked your father.'

'Oh, and before I forget, he sent you this letter. Not sure what it's about but he's in with some developers, rebuilding the township. Maybe they want to buy your land — you can't really say there's a house on it now.'

Ryan frowned. 'It was my home and I grew up there. I don't really want to think about selling. Not yet.'

'Why not? It's going to rack and ruin while

you wait. The tropical climate isn't kind to shanties with the roof caved in.'

'It isn't a shanty.'

'It is now. Ryan, you're building a new life for yourself down here so why would you want to go back? Let it go and you might have enough to afford a small place down here.'

'I've no use for a small place — I want to have my own stables one day.'

'Sure. But maybe you'll have to walk before you can run.'

'I hate that expression — what does it mean, anyway? Did Glen send you here to persuade me?'

'No! God, no, I wouldn't do that. I'm just the messenger — you'll do as you think best.'

Ryan held out his hand for Glen's letter, unsure whether to open it in front of the others or not.

'Come on, then,' Mike said. 'What does he say? Don't keep us in suspense.' He wasn't about to let Ryan read it in private.

The envelope contained just one sheet of paper and Ryan was pleased to see it didn't come from a computer but was written in Glen's generous, rounded hand.

*Dear Ryan,*

*I do hope you've been able to settle with your family in Melbourne. I was so sorry to hear of your uncle's accident and hope he is on the road to recovery. I write to ask if you have any plans for that little place of yours up here?*

(Not that little — Ryan thought — there was the new stable block and enough land for a market garden. Why was everyone so anxious to make him think small?)

*If things are going well for you in Melbourne, I can't see you returning to Canesville any time soon. Gradually, we are rising from the disaster and a lot of rebuilding is taking place. Mike will tell you that my colleagues and I are heavily involved. If you do wish to sell, we will make you a generous offer (for old times' sake if nothing else). But you will need to act promptly before there's any more water damage to get the best possible price.*
*Kind thoughts and very best wishes,*
*Glen Harrison*

Ryan folded the letter and put it in the top pocket of his shirt.
'Come on!' Mike was impatient. 'I did take the trouble to bring it in person. What does Pa have to say?'
'Not much. Just that he wants to buy the

farm. I'll need to think about that.'

'What for?'

'Leave him alone, Michael,' Chrissie said softly. 'Ryan has a mind of his own and doesn't take kindly to being pushed.' She was thinking of her father and his unreasonable dislike of her cousin.

Ryan shot her a grateful smile.

Mike glanced at his watch. 'It's getting late and I must be going. Things to do. People to see.'

'Won't you stay for dinner?' Chrissie said, standing up. 'Mum will be sorry to miss you — '

'Not this time, sweet thing,' he said, setting Ryan's teeth on edge. 'But I have your number — ' patting the mobile phone in his pocket and standing up. 'And I'll be in touch.'

'Will you have time?' Ryan said sharply, hoping to throw a spanner in the works. 'I thought your exams were coming up soon.'

'Nothing serious.' Mike grinned, realizing what his friend was up to. 'Not till the end of the year.'

'I'll see you out,' Ryan said, shepherding him out of the kitchen and walking him briskly towards his car.

'What's got into you?' Mike said. 'You're not yourself at all. Like a different person down here.'

'Well, for starters my uncle hates me — I

180

feel as if I'm walking on eggshells here.'

'All the more reason to sell to my dad and get a place of your own.'

'I'm not ready for that yet. And besides, I can't leave Tommy. He needs me here.'

Mike rolled his eyes. 'It's just a horse, Ryan. A dumb animal doesn't care who looks after it, long as it's fed — '

Ryan shook his head; it was useless to protest: Mike didn't feel the same about animals and would never see his point of view. 'And please, Mike, do me a favour and leave Chrissie alone. She's just come out of a bad long-term relationship and — '

'That's good news, then. She'll be ripe for a new one on the rebound — with me.'

'For the sake of our friendship — please, Mike — lay off. Do this one thing for me.'

Mike laughed. 'Oh, now I get it. I know that look. You've got the hots for the lovely Chrissie yourself. And you don't like to think of me getting a piece of her before you do. Your own cousin.' He tutted annoyingly, wagging his finger. 'Naughty boy.'

'Trust you to drag everything down to your own filthy level,' Ryan said, really angry now.

'Steady on. Only joking. Didn't mean anything by it.'

'It's just that Chrissie's one of the best and I don't want to see you hurt her, that's all.'

'Garn — she knows where it's at. She's older than we are.'

'I'm just saying.'

'Well, don't. She's a lawyer, isn't she? I dare say she knows how to look after herself.' Mike swung into his vehicle — a two-seater sports car of some kind, in pristine condition and smelling of leather, fresh from a showroom. 'And don't forget to think about selling that land. My old man doesn't like to be kept dangling for long.'

* * *

Chrissie was thoughtful after Mike had left. She was no stranger to his type and had not been so taken with him as Ryan thought. She found his brash self-confidence totally un-appealing. Even so, she decided she would go out with him if he called. Having had time to reflect, she realized she had misjudged her cousin; he really was falling in love with her. But, although her own heart was breaking over it, Ryan must see there was no future for them and the easiest way to stifle his affection was to form a temporary relationship with his friend.

She didn't have to wait for long. A day or so later, Mike called, and he arranged to meet her on Saturday evening at Parliament Station in town. She felt mean about it, but she made sure Ryan knew she was making this date and got him to drop her off at the nearest train station. She saw the hurt in his eyes but resolved not to weaken. If he suffered a little pain now, eventually it would be for his own good.

Mike greeted her with a wet and lingering kiss on the lips that she found rather disgusting, although she tried not to show it. She realized, with a jolt of surprise, that there was no chemistry between them at all. Certainly not on her side. His kiss didn't make her heart thump in her chest as it had when she kissed Ryan. But no! She really mustn't let herself think about him. Mike was supposed to be her cure.

He had made a booking at a new restaurant in the centre of the city on the fringes of Chinatown.

'I do hope you like Chinese?' he said, which was rather too late as they were already seated and looking through elaborate, tasselled menus. 'I suppose I should have asked.'

'No, I love it,' she said. 'But in a conservative way. I like prawn crackers, sweet and sour prawns and vegetarian fried rice but I'm not too keen on pork or dishes with too much hot chilli.'

The waiter seemed to know Mike and

greeted him like an old friend and when the food arrived, Chrissie started to enjoy herself. She had been feeling more than a little guilty for using Mike to put Ryan off. Right now he was fishing to find out what was going on in her life.

'I hear you're a lawyer,' he said, 'but not working at present?'

Concisely, she told him the story of the 'almost honeymoon' that nearly took place in Europe and how it had resulted in her getting the sack. She avoided telling him about Tony's death.

'But I can't be sorry,' she said at the end of it. 'That firm has a reputation for using people and spitting them out. In hindsight, I'd have left sooner or later, anyway.'

'So what now? Are you trying to get another job?'

'No. Because the old firm bad-mouthed me all over town. My mother's uncle, who's also a lawyer, tells me it's best to lie low till the fuss dies down. Going to tribunal will only get me a reputation as a troublemaker.'

'But that's not fair. Those people shouldn't be able to ruin a person's life in that way.'

'Ho, no? They have a lot of influence in Melbourne — Sydney too. They can do whatever they like. I just have to wait until they have someone else in their sights. Then I can slip under the radar.'

'And on the personal side you don't have a significant other right now?'

'No.' She frowned at this line of questioning, wondering just how much he'd been told. 'And I'm not at all sure I want one.'

'Go on. A lovely girl like you?'

'I'm not lovely at all. My hips have spread and my nose is too big.'

'I don't like button noses. They make me think of pigs.'

She giggled. 'This food is delicious. Thank you, Mike.'

'Good. Would you like something to follow? They do a great banana fritter.'

Chrissie would. And she drank a lot of delicious green tea, refusing his attempts to ply her with alcohol although she noticed he had an exotic cocktail himself, followed by several shots of neat vodka. When the meal was over and he had paid, he slung an arm around her shoulders and propelled her towards the street. Outside, the fresh air hit him and she felt him stagger.

'Sorry.' He burped and gave her a lopsided grin. 'I'm too pissed to drive you home. You'll have to sleep at my place.'

'No, Michael. I have no intention of sleeping at your place — even if it's not in your bed.'

'Come on, sweet thing. Don't play the innocent. You always knew tonight was going to end up in my bed. After all, I just bought you a big Chinese meal — with dessert.'

'Then I'll pay for my share.' She removed his arm from her shoulders and reached into her purse, pulled out several notes and tucked them into his top pocket. 'I don't have to prostitute myself for the price of a dinner.'

He winced. 'Ooh, you have a wicked turn of phrase.'

'You haven't heard the half of it. I wish I could say I enjoyed myself but I didn't. Goodnight to you, Mike. I'll get a taxi now.' She peered up and down the street, looking for one.

'A taxi?' He sniggered, making himself even less appealing. 'At eleven o'clock on a Saturday night. I don't think so.'

As if giving the lie to his words, a taxi swooped to a stop beside them but before she could take it, a laughing foursome pushed her aside and got in, slamming the door in her face. Chrissie blinked, surprised and shocked by their rudeness.

'Come on, sweet thing.' Mike was trying to take her hand. 'Stop playing hard to get and come back to my place.' If anything, his speech was even more slurred and she cursed herself for staying so late. She should have realized he was drinking too much and made her escape sooner. 'It's only a block or so — we can walk.'

'Mike, forget it.' She disengaged herself and pushed him away. 'I'm not going anywhere else — not with you.'

'Be damned to you, then. You little coldwater fish — frigid as the arctic winds that batter your coastline. I'll bet you don't even know what it's all about. Good luck with Ryan, then. Two novices stumbling about, not knowing what to do — ' And, laughing helplessly at what he saw as his own wit, he lurched away from her and set off down the street.

Chrissie closed her eyes for a few seconds in relief and then set about the serious business of hailing a cab, desperate enough to run into the street and try to flag one down. Finally, as she leaped for the kerb in despair, she heard one pull up behind her with a screech of brakes. She turned, ready to climb in, and then hesitated at the open door.

'Hey, wait a minute. You're not a cab — ' she started to say and gave a small shriek as somebody reached out and grabbed her by the wrist, yanking her roughly inside and slamming the door before taking off at speed.

'No, darl, we're not,' said a gravelly voice. 'But you're coming with us just the same.'

At that time of night in a busy street, it all happened so quickly that no one saw the abduction and Mike Harrison, angry and unused to being rejected, had long since disappeared into the crowd moving up the street.

# 11

'I demand that you let me out at once.' Terrified as she was, Chrissie tried to assert herself.

'Sorry, luv. No can do. We're on the freeway.'

'So I see. Where are you taking me?'

There were two men in the car: the driver and this other one, sitting uncomfortably close to her on the back seat. Both wore army fatigues but neither man was wearing a mask. The driver was young but the man sitting beside her was in his late forties at least. Appearing completely at ease, he smiled at her, showing white, even teeth.

'I said — where are you taking me?' she repeated, trying to conceal her terror.

'Don't worry about it,' he said. 'We'll be there soon.'

Chrissie thought fast. Who in the world would want to abduct her — it didn't make sense. She tried to sound reasonable although this man frightened her: he seemed so calm and assured. 'Look, this is obviously a case of mistaken identity. I don't know who you think I am but you have the wrong girl. My people aren't wealthy. We don't have the sort of money kidnappers want.'

'But if they dig deep enough, they can find it.'

'I doubt it. My father used to be well off but now he's a cripple in a wheelchair. My mother and I are doing our best to hold his business together.'

'Oh, my heart bleeds.' The man mocked her, pressing a hand to his chest.

Although she was scared and breathless, Chrissie forced herself to try again. 'So if you'll just pull off the freeway and let me out at the nearest train station, I'll forget that this ever happened. I won't say anything about it at home and no one will notify the police.'

He applauded gently. 'Nice try.' The man was still smiling but his pale eyes were boring into her, cold as ice. 'But I don't make mistakes. You are Rob Lanigan's daughter, Christalynne, and you're here because I have issues with him.'

For a split second she thought of denying it but her shoulders drooped and she nodded instead. 'Money issues, I suppose?'

'That's between him an' me, luv. And if I know your father, he'll pay us handsomely for your return.'

She laughed shortly. 'If that's what you think, you've been sadly misled. My father and I don't get on. He wouldn't give you so much as the small change in his pockets — not for me.'

'But your mother would.' His tone was sly. 'I've known women who'd give the clothes off their backs to save the life of a child.'

Seeing cars passing close by, she moved without warning and started to bang on the side window, trying to catch the attention of other motorists. 'Help me! Help!' She was trying to scream but the man was twisting her wrist and crushing her painfully against the door so it came out as a scarcely audible squeak.

The younger man who was driving looked at them in the rear-view mirror.

'Everything all right back there?' he said. Chrissie thought he sounded almost as scared as she was.

'No. I can handle it,' the older man said over his shoulder before giving Chrissie a sharp slap on the cheek, making her gasp. It stung rather than hurt but she wasn't used to physical punishment and it shocked her.

'Dad!' The driver was watching them in the rear-view mirror. 'Please don't rough her up. You said you weren't going to harm her.'

'Shut up. Keep your eyes on the road and stop calling me dad,' the older man snapped before lowering his voice and whispering so that only Chrissie should hear. 'Behave yourself. I don't like hurting women but if I have to, I do. Be a good girl now and hide your head under this rug.' He picked it up from the floor and threw it at her. 'I don't want you to see where we're going.'

Chrissie did as she was told. The rug made her feel sick as it was dirty and smelled of some animal, probably a dog, but she didn't want him to hit her again.

Only now did she realize she was in deep trouble. She was dealing with a ruthless man who would show no mercy and stop at nothing. Even if the impossible happened and her father paid up, she didn't think her prospects were good. It seemed unlikely that she would get out of this situation alive.

*　*　*

Ryan was the first person to worry, realizing she hadn't come home. Trying to sound only mildly interested, he questioned Val although his heart was heavy. Since Chrissie wasn't there, making breakfast as usual when he came in after exercising and feeding Tommy, he believed she had stayed in Melbourne with Mike. He had a horrible mental picture of her lying tousled and sated across an enormous king-sized bed.

'No, I haven't heard from her, Ryan.' Val seemed a bit irritated by this line of questioning. 'She's a grown woman and I like to give her some space. She doesn't have to explain herself to me if she chooses to stay at a friend's place overnight.'

'But surely — '

'And I'd much rather she did that than try to drive herself home after a night on the town.'

'She wasn't driving. I took her to catch the train.'

'Fine. And what she's doing now isn't any of my business — or yours,' she said as an afterthought. 'If you must know, I'm pleased that she's starting to get out and about again. I was beginning to worry. She looked to be falling into a depression after what happened to Tony.'

'I just wish she wasn't with Mike. Oh, I know he's my friend and it sounds disloyal to say so, but he has a habit of chasing a girl till he gets her and then discarding her like an old shoe.'

Val laughed. 'And you think your friend is such a Casanova that he can lure Chrissie into his bed in the space of one night? A young man not much older than you are?'

'Age has nothing to do with it. I've watched Mike in action for years. He can turn on the charm when he wants to. And Chrissie's vulnerable right now.'

'I promise you, she's no fool and a lot tougher than you think. She'll see through any superficial charm.'

Ryan sighed. 'I hope you're right.'

'And you'd better stop this or I'll think you've got a crush on her yourself.'

Ryan looked away, cursing the telltale colour that he felt sweeping up from his throat. Fortunately for him, at that moment his bread started burning in the toaster as it was turned up too high, setting off the kitchen smoke alarm. By the time the noise had been stopped with much laughter, napping of tea towels and the barking of Tinka, the awkward moment had been forgotten.

But even Val became anxious when another twenty-four hours passed and there was still no word from Chrissie. She had made coffee and was sitting with Ryan and Margie, the young woman who came in to clean for her twice a week.

'It isn't like her to leave me without word for so long,' Val said. 'She usually checks in to say if she'll be in for dinner or not. You're quite sure, Margie, she didn't leave a message and you forgot to tell me?'

'I never forget your messages, Val.' The girl

looked injured. 'You know me better than that.'

'Sure I do. Sorry.' Val laid a hand on the girl's shoulder. 'It's just that I'm starting to worry.'

'I could call Mike,' Ryan offered, sounding hesitant. 'Find out if he knows where she is.'

'Thank you, Ryan,' Val said. 'You were right to be concerned. We should have started checking before.'

But only an answering service responded at Mike's flat and Ryan had to leave a message, asking him to call back. Mike didn't respond until late on Monday evening, sounding breezy and without a care in the world.

'Hi there,' he said. 'When are you coming in so we can have a night out on the town? There's this great place that's just opened and — '

'Mike, wait. It's about Chrissie — she wouldn't still be with you — would she?' He took a deep breath, hoping the answer would be in the negative.

'That one? Hell, no. She lit out on me right after dinner. I left her hailing a cab.'

'And you didn't wait to see that she got one?'

'No, because she didn't want me to. Feminine equality and all that. It wasn't very late, anyway. If you must know, we had a bit of a disagreement over where she was going to spend the night.'

'Oh? Turned you down, did she?' Ryan's heart was singing.

'Ssh! And don't let it get around — you'll ruin my bad reputation. She's a right little harpy, that one — she gave me the real stink-eye and her acid tongue. She'll make a good lawyer all right. In the olden days she'd be sending good men to the gallows.'

Ryan had to laugh. But when he put down the phone, he didn't feel quite so happy. No one had heard from Chrissie for almost forty-eight hours.

Val was really concerned now although she was trying not to show it — nobody liked a stifling, overprotective mother. But she did start ringing around some of her daughter's old friends, including Michelle. The two girls had once been very close.

'Sorry, Mrs L. I've hardly seen anything of Chrissie lately — I've just come back from overseas. Is she still engaged to that blond fellow — Tony, wasn't it?'

'No, she broke it off a while ago and he's — well, he's not around any more.' Val wanted to avoid the subject of Tony's death.

'Good. I always thought that was an unequal relationship — he stifled her, pulling her down. And the last time I saw her, I said so. That's why we fell out.'

'I'm sorry, Michelle. I thought you were such good friends, you wouldn't let Tony come between you.'

'He monopolized her. Didn't like her seeing anyone else, especially me.'

'So she hasn't been in touch?'

'No. Why, what's happened? Are you saying you don't know where she is?' Michelle was nothing if not direct.

'Not at the moment. No.'

'It's not like Chrissie to play games and disappear. Maybe I shouldn't ask but did you two have a row or something?'

'No, we're very close. There was nothing like that.'

'I'll ask around some of our old mates, if you like. Better coming from me than her mum checking up.'

'Thank you, Michelle — I'd be grateful. It's been more than two days now and I'm beginning to think something's wrong.'

'You're right. It isn't like her. Leave it with me and I'll see what I can find out. In the meantime, maybe you should report her missing.'

Val sighed. 'Oh, I do hope it won't come to that.'

★   ★   ★

Another day was to pass before the kidnappers' note turned up. Robert came bowling into the kitchen in his wheelchair, waving it at Val. Ryan, startled by Robert's unusual arrival downstairs, had just finished breakfast and stood up, ready to leave. He spent as little time as possible around his uncle; an arrangement that suited both of them.

'What d'you make of this?' If anything, Robert sounded more grumpy than usual. 'Came in the post this morning. Says they have Chrissie. I thought she was staying with friends in town?'

'No. She's been missing for several days,' Val said, standing up from the table where she was eating toast.

'And nobody thought to tell me?'

Val shrugged.

'Better read it, then. I thought it might be a joke.' Robert tossed it onto the table. It was a printed note from a computer, brief and to the point.

I need $500,000 in cash for the return of your daughter. You have twenty-four hours to find it and bring it to our old meeting place in the lay-by near Dandenong at midnight tomorrow. Be punctual. If you're not there with the money at midnight tomorrow, the fee will increase in daily increments, the longer you delay. I don't need to sign this — you know who I am. And don't involve the police — it will end badly if you do.

'End badly?' Val finished reading it. 'Rob, this is no joke. I don't like it at all. And what do they mean — our old meeting place? You know who sent this, don't you, Robert.'

'Maybe. There's more than one possibility. I used to meet up with some guys who sold imported drugs from the US — a lay-by at night off the highway near Dandenong. An excellent place to meet away from prying eyes.'

'Heavens, Rob.' Val was struggling to digest this news. 'How long have you been doing this — taking illicit drugs?'

'They weren't for me, stupid. Performance-enhancing drugs for the horses. New on the market and quite undetectable. Get past any test.'

'But that's horrible. You never told me you were experimenting with drugs on our horses.'

'No, o'course not. If you knew nothing, you'd have no trouble playing the innocent if the authorities got wind of it and came sniffing around.'

'Rob, that's so irresponsible. Those drugs are illegal because they haven't been fully tested. No one knows what the long-term effects might be on the horses.'

'Oh, spare me. You'll be joining Animal Rights next. How many times must I tell you, there's no room for sentiment in this business. Horses are raised for the racing industry — to be useful only so long as they can run. Just a commodity between the racetrack, the abattoir and the cat's meat factory.'

'How can you be so callous?' Val's shoulders slumped. 'I thought you loved our horses as I do. I never realized that's how you thought of them.'

'Well, now you do. Maybe it's time you faced up to some of the realities of life. And if you're wondering why we haven't had so many in the winners' circle lately, it's not through any lack of skill in our training regime but because I can't drive out at night to meet our supplier.'

Val watched him, considering this for a moment before giving a mirthless laugh and shaking her head.

'No, Rob, you're lying. I don't buy that story at all — it's a total fabrication and doesn't make sense. If you had such a sweet arrangement with these people before, why should they ruin it all by taking Chrissie? Drug smugglers don't like to draw attention to themselves. But obviously you've upset someone. So what did you do?'

'I dunno. They're not regular business people, they're part of the underworld. Anyway, they could be bluffing. If we ignore them, they'll realize it's not going to work and let her go.'

'I won't risk it, Rob. By the tone of that note, these people mean business and we have to take them seriously.'

'How? I don't have thousands of dollars stashed in my bottom drawer.'

'Nobody does. But you have shares, don't you? You must sell some.'

'Now?' Robert frowned. 'It's hardly the best time — '

'I don't care. I'll sell my jewellery too if it means we can have Chrissie home safe.'

'You will not. That's family treasure — bought as a hedge against hard times.'

'Well, they're not going to get much harder than this, are they? Silly me, I always thought those jewels were mine.'

Robert glared at her.

'There's no point in arguing, Rob. Somehow we have to pull that money together and quickly — you can see what they're saying about delay — '

'Slow down a minute. I need to think about this.'

'Robert, you're not hearing me. This is about Chrissie's safety — '

'Yes but how do we know they won't take the money and leave her body lying in a ditch?'

Val flinched at the callousness of the remark. 'We don't. But they won't want to be hunted as murderers, will they? It's the money they're after. Soon as they have it — they'll let her go.'

'Oh, sure. You'd like to think so. Long as she can identify them she's a danger. Why should they let her go?'

'We have to trust them whether you like it or not.' Val was becoming close to tears. 'And this last dig. What do they mean by that?' Val tapped the note which was lying on the table. ' 'I don't need to sign this — you know who I am.' Who are these people, Rob? And what do they have against you? I think you know a whole lot more than you're telling me.'

'All right. I had a special arrangement with this guy — an ex-marine or commando — I dunno. Everything was fine for a while but last time things didn't go according to plan so I refused to pay.'

'Now it begins to make sense. So what kind of special arrangement did you have with this ex-commando? What unpleasant task did you set him that you wouldn't do for yourself?'

'Stop it, woman. You're relentless. All you need to know is that he's harder to control than I expected.'

'So we must pay him off and get rid of him. We don't need someone like that in our lives.'

'I have a better plan. You take a suitcase to the lay-by filled with old newspapers. And when they meet you there, ready to collect, we'll have the police waiting for them ready to pounce — '

'The police aren't your private army, Rob. We've been told not to involve them and I won't have Chrissie put at risk. There's no way out of it. We have to pay up and do exactly as these people ask.'

Ryan spoke up softly for the first time. He had been leaning quietly against the stove listening to everything that had gone before. Their conversation had been very revealing but although he was angered by some of Robert's sentiments, he knew he would learn more if he kept silent and didn't interrupt. He was like the invisible man; both Val and Robert had quite forgotten he was there.

'I'll do it,' he said. 'Let me take the money and go to the lay-by to deliver it. They don't know me but they probably know enough to recognize your car. I'll hand over the case with the money in exchange for Chrissie and we'll be out of there.'

'If only it would turn out to be that simple,' Val said. 'Thank you, Ryan, but I'll have to do it. I can't let you put yourself in danger for us.'

'Whyever not?' Robert sounded falsely hearty, eyes suddenly glistening. 'That's a great idea. Ryan is younger and stronger than we are. He'll fare better than either of us if anything goes wrong.'

'That's settled, then,' Ryan said.

# 12

Although Robert was still planning to cheat the kidnappers by placing money-sized packets of newspaper under a shallow layer of banknotes, Val wouldn't hear of it. She had sold nearly all her jewellery aside from pieces of sentimental value and only then would he sell some shares to make up the difference. He still wanted to argue about paying them at all.

'It's stupid to let them have what they want without a fight,' he grumbled. 'It leaves us with nowhere to go. Give in too easily and they could demand even more.'

'We can cross that bridge when we come to it, Rob. I'm not taking any chances with Chrissie's safety.' So saying, Val turned her back on him to count the money one last time, making sure it was all there. She closed the briefcase with a snap and handed it to Ryan. 'All our hopes and wishes go with you, Ryan. Don't take any more risks than you need to.'

'I won't,' he said, giving her a quick hug, sensing that she felt as keyed up and tense as he did. They'd agreed he should take her little Subaru to the rendezvous — it was newer and nippier than the old yellow taxi they used to carry Robert around. The vehicle he had taken to Queensland was a write-off after the accident in Sydney and, as yet, Val hadn't found the courage to tell him he was unlikely to regain the use of his legs or drive except in a specially modified car. He was still expecting to make a complete recovery.

Ryan wanted to set off early, hoping to gain an advantage by being there before the kidnappers arrived.

'I still think I should go with you,' Val said, holding on to the keys until the last possible minute. 'I don't like sending you into danger alone.'

'Leave it be, Val.' Robert smirked, eyes glittering. 'Most lads enjoy a bit of danger at his age. It'll be quite an adventure for him.'

Some adventure! Ryan thought. I'll be relieved when it's all over and I have Chrissie safe. Aloud he said, 'No, Val. You stay here as backup. If I run into trouble, you might need to involve the cops.' Clearly, he didn't trust Robert to alert them. 'I'll have my hands full, getting Chrissie away from them. I don't need you there as another target.'

'Ryan, take care. Just give them the money and call me the instant you have Chrissie safe and they're gone. Oh, poor girl. She must be terrified.'

'Try not to worry,' he said. 'I'll have her home soon.' As he said this, he was hoping his words didn't sound as hollow to Val as they did to him. They both knew there was still a lot to go wrong.

Driving towards Dandenong, he had time to go over all that had happened and wonder about Robert's state of mind. It struck him that the old man wasn't as concerned as a father ought to be — it was Val who was worried sick. And there was something odd about Robert's attitude, too. He seemed excited — almost gleeful that he, Ryan, should volunteer for this dangerous mission. Left to his thoughts as he drove closer to the lay-by where he was to meet the kidnappers, he had time to mull over all that had gone before. He felt certain Robert knew a lot more about these people than he was saying and had to be holding something back. The Lanigans might be comfortably off, but were still far from wealthy so why should they become a target for kidnappers? This was about more than the money or it didn't make sense. He agreed with Val and didn't believe Robert's story that he was buying performance-enhancing drugs for the horses. Ryan spent most of his time in the stables and had never seen anyone giving injections aside from their registered vet. No. Robert had made up this dramatic and shocking story because he was hiding something a lot worse.

★ ★ ★

Chrissie had plenty of time to get to know her captors. It worried her that they didn't trouble to disguise themselves. If they didn't care if she recognized them, releasing her might not be a part of their plan and that wasn't a comforting thought. Shortly before the journey ended, she noted a steep climb on a dirt road with many turns and with gravel crunching beneath the wheels, indicating an unmade country road. When she was allowed to set aside the suffocating rug, she could see they had arrived at a small log cabin buried high in the hills. But which hills? There were several ranges to choose from around Melbourne and it could be any one of them. There seemed to be dense forest all around them and she could see no street lamps or lights nearby to indicate neighbours. She had lost all sense of time and couldn't judge how long it had taken to get there. They had grabbed her purse and tossed her mobile phone out onto the motorway. She felt lost and isolated without it.

The facilities of the cabin were old but, mercifully, clean and although most of what she was given to eat was fast food, brought in by the younger of the two men, there was plenty of it. They didn't intend her to starve.

The older man went out often, leaving the two young people alone although he always insisted on handcuffing her to the brass rail of her bed before doing so, laughing at her promises that she wouldn't try to escape. He had a low opinion of women, she thought.

The younger man, still in his late teens, was more friendly and liked to chat, so it was easy for her to draw him out, getting him to talk about himself. He told her his name was Tim and the older man was his father, although they didn't find each other until he was a teenager. He had always believed his father was dead until his mother told him how to find him when she found she was diagnosed with ovarian cancer in its later stages. She didn't have much time; her death was sudden, taking place with a speed that shocked him. Chrissie could see that it upset him to speak of her still; his voice grew husky and tears came readily to his eyes. He blew his nose into a crumpled tissue and continued his tale after taking a shuddering breath.

'Harry didn't want to believe I was his, not at first,' he said. 'He's always been a loner with no real friends — an odd sort who didn't trust anyone. He told me he didn't need a son to look after, dragging him down. But he only had to look in the mirror to see I was speaking the truth. There I was — a younger version of himself. We got on all right but he still didn't want me around, said I was cramping his lifestyle — with girls, I suppose. So I got shoved off to boarding school, 'to do some more growing up', so he said. God, how I hated that place. They had us bellowing hymns all day and didn't teach us anything. The food was miserable too — macaroni cheese and stodgy puddings to fill us up. Most of us were spotty and overweight. Soon as I could, I learned to drive and make myself useful to him so he'd let me leave.'

'Didn't you want an education, Tim?' Chrissie said. An enthusiastic student herself, she found it hard to understand anyone who didn't like to study.

'Not if it meant staying at that school.' He wrinkled his nose.

'So what is your father teaching you now?' She couldn't resist teasing him. 'To be a good criminal? Kidnapping is quite an advanced place to start. Higher up the ladder than shoplifting lollies. He'll have you robbing banks next.'

'No, he won't.' The young man looked uncertain. 'This kidnapping is a one-off. He said so.'

'And you believed him?' she said, speaking softly to make him lean closer. 'Are you up for murder as well, Tim? Remember, I've seen enough to identify both of you. D'you honestly think your father will let me go?'

'Yes, of course. When he gets the money. He told me so.' Tim blushed, looking shocked. 'He doesn't like doing this — it's only out of necessity because a man cheated him.'

'That would be my father, I suppose?'

The lad shrugged. 'I dunno. He doesn't tell me much. He has nothing against you. It's only the money he wants — for us to make a new start. A new life for ourselves overseas.'

'Oh?' she said softly. 'And where will that be?'

Tim paused, staring at her and breathing heavily, realizing he'd already said too much. 'I don't want to talk to you any more. Dad said I shouldn't, anyway. In case I give too much away.'

'Too late, Tim,' she said softly. 'You're already on the slippery slope.'

'Stop it,' he said. 'You're frightening me.'

'Be afraid, Tim,' she said. 'Be very afraid. Your father's a ruthless man and I think he means to kill me.'

He left her then, slamming the door behind him.

She knew it was a slim chance but it was the best she could do; plant the seeds of doubt with Tim concerning his father's intentions and hope that he would refuse to let himself be a party to murder.

On the way back down the mountain, she had been forced to lie under that smelly rug yet again and when the car stopped, she sat up, pushing it aside and blinking as her eyes became used to the light. They were in a deserted lay-by with traffic moving on a busy freeway nearby.

'Where are we?' she said. 'There's nobody here.'

'For your sake, there had better be.' Sitting uncomfortably close to her, Harry gave her a little shake. For the first time she sensed that he too was nervous, breathing heavily and smelling of fresh perspiration. 'Because if anyone tries to play the hero and cheat me, somebody's going to get hurt.'

Chrissie knew this was no idle threat and when it occurred to her that she was likely to die anyway, somehow she was no longer scared. She could only hope that when death came, it would be swift and painless.

'Don't expect my father to be there.' She was suddenly flippant. 'He's stuck in a wheelchair — quite aside from being a devout coward. Well, you probably know that already.

No. He'll send my mother. So please don't hurt her — I know she won't try to cheat you. Promise me you'll just take the money and go.'

'You talk too much. And stop telling me what to do — I don't like it.' Harry glared at her through narrowed eyes. 'All bets are off until I have the money. That's the only way you and your mum will get out of here.' He gave her another shove to emphasize his words. 'Just remember I'm armed.' And he showed her the revolver before tucking it into his belt at the back; a gesture so practised that she knew he was used to handling firearms.

Chrissie smiled. Beyond fear now, she was almost resigned to her fate. Her only hope was that Val wouldn't have to share it. 'Here she comes. That's my mother's car. Right on time, isn't she?'

Ordering Tim to stay in the driver's seat and wait, Harry pulled up his grey hoodie so that his face was hidden. Then he got out of the car, opened the back door and pulled Chrissie out where she could be seen. He held her arm in a vice-like grip, far from gentle.

'Here she is,' he called out. 'Your daughter, safe and sound.'

★ ★ ★

Ryan watched their unsteady approach before getting out of the car to meet them. There seemed to be something familiar about this man but as yet he couldn't place him. Perhaps it was the grey hoodie. They were common enough — worn by men and boys everywhere. But this man seemed unusually tall and with a strange, loping walk. Ryan was sure he had seen him before.

It came to him in a flashback — a scene from the past. This was the man who had been snooping around the stables up north before Ryan's world changed forever — before his father died, before the horror of the cyclone and the tree fell on his mother. Intuitively, he knew that this man was responsible for more than a few of his woes. And now he was threatening and terrorizing Chrissie, the woman he loved.

A cold fury took hold of him as he got out of the car, pulling the briefcase with him. He set off towards them, mouth set, not yet knowing what he would do.

'Don't come any closer, Ryan,' Chrissie called, warning him. 'He has a gun.'

At this crucial moment, a huge logistics truck left the highway and pulled up with a squeal of airbrakes behind them, headlights lighting up the whole scene.

Realizing it was impossible to hide now,

Harry gave Chrissie a vicious shove, making her gasp and fall to her knees, bruising them on the rough surface of the road. Pain prevented her from moving right away.

'Put the briefcase down and move away,' he ordered Ryan. 'We have to act quickly now there's a witness. Don't make this worse than it is already.'

But Ryan was beyond reason now and kept coming. Only then did Harry pull the gun, releasing the safety catch and aiming it at Ryan's heart.

'No,' Chrissie said brokenly. 'Please, no.'

Ryan ignored the order, still moving forward as Harry lowered the gun and fired it into the ground near his feet.

The truck driver didn't wait to see any more. He started his vehicle again and charged past them, peppering them with gravel as he did so. Continuing to keep his firearm trained on Ryan, Harry grinned.

'That's what I like to see,' he said as the truck barged onto the highway, causing a fanfare of horns as other drivers were forced to move out of his way. 'A man who doesn't want to get involved. And you keep your distance,' he said to Ryan. 'Next time, I'll aim for your head.'

At this point Tim disobeyed his father's instructions and got out of the car to come running towards them. He too sounded distraught.

'Dad, you told me the gun wasn't loaded. You said it was only for show.'

'Shut up and get back in the car, Tim.' Harry glanced at him, momentarily distracted.

Ryan took advantage of this to hurl the briefcase with all the force he could muster, directly at Harry's chest. It burst open on contact, scattering money around them like a game-show bonanza of wealth.

Harry, winded and startled, still managed to hang on to the gun but Ryan was upon him now, trying to wrestle it from his grasp. Although Harry was more used to unarmed combat, age was catching up on him and he wasn't as agile as he thought. He was no match for Ryan, who was young and whose arms were unusually strong from a lifetime spent exercising and controlling horses. Try as he may, Harry couldn't break Ryan's hold on the gun as they struggled to gain control of it.

Suddenly, the firearm went off again and the two men froze for a moment as Chrissie screamed. Almost certainly one of them had been hit.

By this time, a Highway Patrol car had come on the scene, sirens wailing, probably summoned by the truck driver, who had been appalled by the drama unfolding before him.

Although there was blood on both of them, it was Harry who sagged in Ryan's grasp and collapsed to the ground. Tim knelt beside him, sobbing and using his hands to try and stop the blood flowing up between his fingers from the wound in his father's chest. Harry had taken a bullet at very close range.

'God — oh, God, get an ambulance. Don't let him die!' Tim pleaded with Ryan who stood rooted to the spot staring down at them, equally shocked. 'You did this, you bastard! You shot my father.'

Ryan shook his head. 'No, no. The gun just went off. I don't know who pulled the trigger.'

Grim-faced, two policemen emerged from their vehicle, assessing the scene. One of them was quick to retrieve the revolver, placing it carefully in a plastic bag. By this time another squad car with two more policemen had arrived as backup.

By now an ambulance had also arrived at the scene. When Harry, now barely conscious, had been stabilized sufficiently to load into it with Tim and the paramedics beside him, it took off at speed, sirens blaring.

The police quickly gathered up the money and pushed it back into the briefcase.

Ryan had his arms around Chrissie's

shoulders and he could feel her whole body still shaking as she put an arm round his waist to steady herself.

'You're quite sure you're not hurt?' she whispered. 'When that gun went off, I was certain you must be dead.'

'Oh, it takes a lot to kill me,' Ryan said uncertainly, enjoying her concern.

'Ahem — sorry to break up the touching reunion.' It was the police sergeant who spoke, regarding them both with suspicion. 'But a man has been seriously injured here and we have to find out who owns this.' He held up the gun in the plastic bag.

'It belongs to the man who was shot,' Chrissie said.

'We'll need statements from both of you so you'd better accompany us to the station — now.' The sergeant was unimpressed by her outburst. 'You can lock up your car and leave it where it is.'

'Wait a minute,' Chrissie said. 'You're behaving as if we're the criminals here. Those people are kidnappers and I was their victim. The money in that briefcase belongs to my parents. They raised it to ransom me.'

'Really?' The policeman looked sceptical. 'How do I know that's the truth? That it isn't a piece of quick thinking on your part to cover up a drug deal gone wrong? We're dealing with things like this all the time, especially around here — '

'If that's what you think — where's the dope?' Chrissie said. 'I don't have it and neither does he.' She nodded towards Ryan.

'Could be in the ambulance with the injured guy. Or the truck driver.' The policeman smiled. 'People are good at finding ways to dump anything incriminating when the police turn up.'

After all they'd been through, Chrissie groaned, feeling close to tears.

'Why can't you believe me?' she said. 'Talk to my parents. Please. They'll tell you I'm speaking the truth.'

'Give us your phone, then.'

She patted her pockets, forgetting she'd lost it. 'I can't,' she said. 'The kidnappers threw it away.'

'I have mine,' Ryan said, producing it.

'Fine.' The policeman confiscated it. 'You're still coming with us. We can call your relatives from the station.'

Exhausted after all they'd been through, Chrissie and Ryan sat in the police car holding hands; for now, they were just relieved to be safe and didn't want to say too much within the hearing of the officers. Unfortunately for them, that particular lay-by had been the scene of many a drug deal and the local police were used to catching both users and dealers there.

At the station, Ryan and Chrissie were interviewed separately and were finally allowed to make a phone call to Val, who arrived in a borrowed car an hour or so later. Although the policemen had been unwilling at first to let go of their drug-dealing theory, Val's anger soon convinced them otherwise.

'My daughter has been through enough already without being treated like a criminal,' she ranted. 'And this young man is my nephew.' She indicated Ryan. 'I can vouch for him, too. You need to let these young people go.'

'Your daughter can leave,' the sergeant said. 'She has no charges to answer. But not the young man.'

'Why not?'

'Because we've had word from the hospital that the man who was shot has just died. And if the weapon used in the shooting turns out to belong to your nephew — '

'But it doesn't, Officer. It belongs to the kidnapper,' Chrissie said. 'Ask the truck driver, he saw what happened — or most of it. Speak to the boy who went to the hospital with the kidnapper — he's his son. Tim's really just a kid. He isn't a criminal like his father — not yet anyway.'

'These matters will all be investigated — in due course. For now, Ryan Lanigan must remain in custody. He could be facing a charge of murder.'

'He was trying to rescue me — to protect me,' Chrissie pleaded, once more close to tears. 'Why can't you believe me?'

'Come on, Chrissie,' Val whispered. 'They're not going to change their minds now. We need to get in touch with Uncle Henry — see what he can do.'

Val's uncle Henry was a sharp mind; an elderly lawyer who still had a practice, although it was mostly run by his junior partners. He would know what to do in this situation. She had the feeling that the police, cheated of an open-and-shut case of drug dealing, would like to pursue the charge of murder instead.

# 13

When Chrissie and her mother arrived home, instead of hiding in his study as usual, Robert was waiting for them downstairs. He pulled the front door open, the moment he heard their approach.

'Come on, then, tell me what happened,' he said, scarcely glancing at Chrissie. He made no move to embrace her or even to ask how she felt after such an ordeal. Instead, he pulled a face and recoiled, waving his hand as if there was a bad smell under his nose. 'Christ, but you reek! You need to get a shower.'

'So would you, if you'd been held in one room for nearly a week and scarcely allowed to go to the bathroom.' She was close to tears, her emotions still raw and close to the surface, and she was in no mood for criticism.

'So, since you're here in one piece and unharmed, everything must have gone according to plan?'

'Not exactly,' Val sighed, remembering that he didn't yet know the whole story. He had been upstairs in his study when she took the call from the police station. In a panic because she had no transport as the old yellow taxi had gone to be serviced, she was forced to borrow a car from a stable hand who had come in to work early. He wasn't happy about lending his car to a woman on the verge of hysteria but she left him no choice; she was the boss's wife, after all. It had been a long night for everyone and Val could think only of sleep but now she must stay awake long enough to tell Robert the whole sorry tale.

'Go on, then. What happened?' he said, raising his voice. 'Did Ryan give them the money?'

'If you'll stop yelling for a moment, I'll tell you.' Val was in no mood for one of his tantrums and after all the drama, the adrenaline had worn off and she was exhausted. 'But first I need some tea or a stiff drink — probably both.'

Impatient with her father's line of questioning, Chrissie pushed past him, steering Val towards the kitchen where the fire in the Aga was still in, keeping the room warm.

'I'll make some tea and then you can get to bed for an hour or so,' she whispered. 'It's too late now but you'll need to talk to Uncle Henry first thing in the morning.'

'What do you need Henry for?' Robert demanded, following in the wheelchair, angry at being ignored. 'And where's the boy?'

'Finally,' Chrissie said, turning to look at him. 'I thought you'd never ask.'

'What happened, then? Is he injured? In hospital?' Robert seemed more eager than anxious. 'He isn't dead?'

'Of course Ryan isn't dead.' Val glared at him. 'What gave you that idea? But he is in trouble. The police were involved and they're holding him because one of the kidnappers was shot and they're not sure how it happened. And to make matters worse, the man died on the way to the hospital.'

'So what are you saying? That Ryan shot Harry?' Robert whispered, eyes glittering as he absorbed this news. With Harry dead and gone, most of his troubles would be over.

'It wasn't like that.' Chrissie closed her eyes against the unwelcome memory. 'Dad, we've been through hell in these last few hours. Can we talk about this in the morning?'

'No, we can't,' Robert insisted. 'I'll pour us all a shot of whisky and you'll tell me everything. Now!'

Val and Chrissie looked at each other and sighed. Robert wasn't going to let them rest until he had a full account of the night's events. All the same, he listened impatiently, scarcely able to wait until Chrissie reached the end of her tale.

'So, if you don't have the briefcase and the kidnapper's dead, who has my money now?'

'Our money,' Val reminded him gently.

'Who do you think?' Chrissie said, irritated that his concern appeared to be more for the missing money than for his nephew's return. 'The police, of course. They're holding it as evidence, their favourite theory being that it was money involved in a drug deal gone bad.'

'Then you get old Henry down there first thing in the morning and set them straight,' Robert growled. 'I'll go myself if I have to.'

'I'm sure we can manage without you, Dad.' Chrissie sighed. 'I'm having a long, hot shower now and then I'm looking forward to sleeping in my own bed.'

★   ★   ★

The old yellow taxi was returned before nine the next morning and Robert insisted on going to the police station with them although Val tried to persuade him otherwise. She had spoken to her uncle, who wanted to meet them before they confronted the police, to make sure they were all on the same page. They were already on the road when Sir Henry called to say he had been delayed. He told them not to go into the police station on their own but to wait for him on a bench in the street outside. He apologized yet again and said he would be there as soon as he could.

'If I'd known he was going to be so late, I'd have had breakfast before we left,' Robert grumbled, having no patience to wait for anyone. 'That old fool should learn to get out of bed in the morning. Maybe it's time we hooked up with a younger man with more modern ideas.' He shivered. 'And it's chilly out here.'

'I did tell you not to come,' Val said, irritated by her husband's criticism. 'And my uncle may be old but his mind is as sharp as ever. I trust him implicitly because he's the best there is. And I'm sure he'll have a good reason for being late.'

He did. Arriving just over an hour later, Sir Henry apologized yet again. A distinguished little man with grey hair in a style he had worn for years, neatly trimmed moustache and old-fashioned clothes, Val had always thought he looked like a forties film star. He exuded confidence and she began to feel better already now he was here, taking charge. He hugged both Chrissie and Val but scarcely acknowledged the man in the wheelchair — in fact he seemed surprised to see him at all. There had never been any affection lost between them. Henry knew just how much of Robert's prosperity was owed to Val's inheritance from her father and he enjoyed cutting the younger man down to size.

'I would have been here sooner,' he said. 'But I wanted my contacts to do some research on the man who was shot. And when they started digging, there was plenty to find. Ex-military gone bad — as they sometimes do — and operating under more than one alias. Psychiatric issues combined with a complete lack of remorse; a man who enjoyed killing. Getting paid for it was just the cherry on the cake. You were lucky to get away from him, Chrissie — he didn't often leave witnesses around to identify him. And he had three surnames — Green, Brown or Black, with a passport to match each identity. A hired killer who covered his tracks very well so it took us a while to put it together today.'

'But how did you manage to do it so quickly?' Val said.

'Oh, I have my sources.' He smiled. 'And I had some luck. His son was ingenuous enough to give their present address to the hospital. Yes, yes — I know all about privacy laws but there are ways around that. I spoke to Tim this morning and understandably he's distraught. Harry was the only relative he had left. I'm afraid I took advantage of his misery to get to the bottom of their recent activities. He was only too ready to pour his heart out to a sympathetic ear.'

'Tim isn't a criminal, Uncle,' Chrissie put in. 'Just rather naive. I don't think he realized the extent of his father's activities or how far he was prepared to go. He knew only that his father had issues with mine — hence the abduction. Harry convinced him the payment was owed and justified.'

'I still think he should rot in jail,' Robert said. 'His father's a common criminal and the boy an accessory to a kidnapping that could have escalated to murder. I shall press charges.'

'I'd think carefully before doing that, Rob,' Henry said. 'The police might already be wondering how you came to the attention of such a man, in spite of the low profile he managed to keep. Awkward questions may be asked. I'd play the innocent, if I were you — '

'No!' Robert smote the arms of his chair in frustration. 'I want to see justice done! And I want my money back, too.'

'Calm down,' Henry said, unimpressed by this show of temper. 'Justice has already been done — the man is dead. My best advice would be for you and Val to tell the police you have no idea why your family has been targeted in this way. Nothing like it has ever happened before. As for the boy — forget him — he'll have trouble enough getting on with his life after this. Let him go.'

'Dad, listen to me.' Chrissie had to speak up, crouching by his chair to look into his face. 'I'm the one who was kidnapped and I spent a lot of time with Tim. He isn't a bad kid and he's already suffered enough. His mother is dead and losing his father is going to leave him in pieces. What good will it do to send him to jail? He might not be a criminal now but he'll learn enough to embrace a life of crime by the time he gets out.'

'Trust you to put a sentimental spin on it,' Robert sneered, leaning away from her.

'Come on,' Henry said. 'We can argue about all this later. Right now I have to convince the cops that your nephew isn't a criminal and they should let him go.'

This didn't happen easily. The police were disappointed to have their drug-dealing theories blown out of the water, but they couldn't get past the persuasive arguments of Henry Wheeler. He soon worked his magic and Ryan was allowed to leave the police station without being charged, although he was warned not to leave the state and to remain at his current address. All the same, the police were in no hurry to release him and all this took until mid-afternoon. There would be an inquest into the death of Harry Green, as his son had named him, and Ryan would be needed to give evidence at the very least. Sir Henry left, promising to keep an eye on any developments. Robert continued to object because his briefcase containing the money was to remain in police custody for the time being, but his complaints fell on deaf ears.

Fortunately, Val's car was still at the lay-by where they left it. Happy to avoid Robert's company, Ryan offered to drive it home, pleased when Chrissie volunteered to accompany him. Meanwhile, Val had to drive her disgruntled husband in the old taxi, forced to listen to his catalogue of complaints. Having missed two meals, he said he was starving and made her stop on the way home to buy fish and chips. Then he proceeded to devour them greedily from the paper, filling the car with the smell of fried fish and cooking oil. From time to time, Val glanced at him in the rear-view mirror. You'll keep, old fella, she thought. You think you've got away with everything, but you're wrong. There are some very big holes in your story and I'll have some very pertinent questions for you when we get home.

★ ★ ★

Alone with Chrissie for the first time in a very long while, Ryan was suddenly shy, not knowing what to say to her as they joined the freeway, travelling home. She saved him the trouble by speaking up first.

'Ryan, I haven't thanked you properly for what you did last night. You put yourself in danger and took a tremendous risk for me.'

'Think nothing of it, Chrissie. Anyone who loved you would have done the same.'

'Oh Ryan, I wish you wouldn't keep saying those things. It's too painful when you know it can't come to anything. I will always be your friend but there mustn't be a romantic attachment between us.'

'But it's there, Chrissie, whether we want it or not. We're not brother and sister, we're cousins, that's all. And now we have some time to ourselves without other people, I need to talk to you properly without any intrusions. And I don't think I can do that while I'm driving.' So saying he moved into the left lane and started signalling, ready to leave the freeway.

'Ryan. You're just making things worse for both of us. We need to get home.'

Ignoring her protests, Ryan came off the busy highway and looked around for somewhere secluded to park. He didn't really know this suburb but he had chosen well if he wanted a quiet place to talk. There was a stand of ancient pines lining the road and he was able to pull off and park in a lay-by beside them.

'Now, then,' he said, turning to face her. 'Tell me again why you can't or won't let me love you. Is it really because you can't stand the sight of me?'

'How could you think that? No!' she said, forced to laugh at the directness of his approach. 'But it's wrong for so many reasons, I don't even know where to start.'

'OK. Name them. I'll bet I can shoot them all down in flames.'

'In the first place, you're too young. You're not even twenty-one and I'm twenty-six — '

'Wrong already. I had a birthday last week.'

'Oh, Ryan, why didn't you say something?'

'Because it was the same day you disappeared and I didn't feel like celebrating. I suppose the next thing you'll say is that I'm a bad prospect. A stable hand with no money — '

'Give me a break. That's the last thing that would matter to me.'

'Good,' he said. 'Because it turns out that I might have some money, after all. Glen Harrison — Mike's father — wants to make me an offer for the old farm up north.'

'I didn't know you wanted to sell it.'

'Nor did I, until all this happened with you. I'll never go back and live there again. Not if it means I have to leave Tommy — and you.'

'Oho — I see you put Tommy first.'

'Only to tease you. Oh, Chrissie, I'm so in love with you that it hurts. And I know I'll never love anyone else, not if I live to be a hundred.'

'And I'd be 106 — '

'Don't make fun of me. If you really can't love me, I'll have to accept it but don't make a trivial thing of it, please.'

'Look, I'm not denying that what you're feeling is real — '

'I have no doubt about it. But you keep dodging the question. You still haven't told me how you feel.'

'Because I have to be the voice of reason. Think, Ryan! Think it through before we get carried away on this tide of emotion. We're first cousins, which is the largest stumbling block. We're just too closely related.'

'And if we weren't related at all, could you love me, then?'

'Don't go there, please. Just don't ask.'

'I will. I'll go on asking you all day and all night until I have your answer because you still haven't said no.'

'All right, for all the good it will do you. I feel the same as you do. I've fought it because

I didn't want to face it but I've loved you since the day you kissed me so clumsily on the way home from the races.'

'Yess!' he cried, punching the air. 'She loves me and I want the whole world to hear and celebrate with me.'

'The world won't want to celebrate at all, I can assure you,' she said with a wry smile.

'Then we shan't tell them. We don't have to go public or even get married. We'll just be together in secret. Like this.' And slowly, still expecting resistance, he put his arm around her, drawing her close. He kissed her gently, experimentally until, sensing her relaxing into the kiss, he deepened it. Chrissie could only think how good it felt as she gave herself up to it with a small sigh. A long time later, flushed and breathless, they had to come up for air.

'Ryan, wait. I don't want to hide in corners, pretending this isn't happening. But if we do marry, it's only natural for us to want children. And as we're so closely related, there could be health issues. Wouldn't it ruin everything if we had to watch a child go through life with a major disability, knowing it was our fault?'

'You're imagining the worst possibility — looking on the darkest side. Why not look on the brighter side? We're healthy — all our parents were healthy.' He closed his eyes briefly, trying to blot out the memory of his mother and the illness that haunted her final days. He gave a small sigh. 'I can't do it, Chrissie. I can't imagine my life without you. Not now.'

'We need to think about this a lot more. I'll talk to my doctor and see what she says concerning the risks.'

'Then you are willing to consider a future with me?'

'I'm making no promises, Ryan. You have to be patient.'

And with that, he had to be content.

Seeing no reason to hurry home only to be bombarded with still more questions from Robert, they found a seafood restaurant willing to serve them an early meal. Chrissie used Ryan's phone to text Val, telling her of their plans so she wouldn't think they had wrapped her car around a tree. It was only when the food was put in front of them that they realized they were starving. Like lovers in a comedy romance, they fed each other oysters with lemon and chilli sauce. Chrissie said she'd never been able to enjoy them before. They sat talking for hours, only now learning how much they had in common; their love of animals, especially horses. Chrissie was a dedicated film buff and loved old black and white movies; she promised to show him some of her favourites. They ate a dessert of chocolate mousse, discovering a shared addiction to chocolate, too. Only after they had lingered over coffee and thin chocolate mints did they reluctantly decide to go home.

Once again, they stopped on the way to indulge their desire for closeness. And this time their lovemaking might have reached a conclusion but for the restrictions of a small car. Time passed without their realizing it and it was well into the evening before they finally arrived home.

# 14

Earlier, on reaching home, Val knew she must confront her husband and raise the various issues that troubled her. Margie was somewhere in the house, wielding the vacuum cleaner for a last go round before she went home, but otherwise they were alone.

In a previous life she would have hesitated, daunted by her husband's size as well as his uncertain temper, but since his accident, he was far less intimidating. He seemed to sense that she had something to say as he headed for the lift as soon as he was back in his chair, hoping to escape to his study before she followed him there.

'What do you want, Val? I'm too busy to talk to you now.' He scowled as she pushed herself into the narrow lift beside him. 'I've wasted enough time today already and need to catch up on my paperwork.'

'What paperwork? Nothing that can't wait, I'm sure,' she said, wanting to remind him that she herself dealt with most of the business of the stables these days. Robert had become so inattentive and careless of late that several owners had lost faith in the Lanigan stables and taken their horses away. Val had to work hard to convince other clients not to follow suit and it was only her heartfelt promises and the memory of her father's good reputation that persuaded them to stay. Blissfully unaware of this close call, Robert thought it was business as usual. He had no idea that the success of the stables now depended largely on Ryan and Tommy. Exasperated by his high-handed attitude she felt bound to tell him so.

'You have no idea, have you, how hard we all work to keep things going here. You don't appreciate anything Ryan does.'

Robert gave a derisive snort. 'He has a roof over his head. What more does he want? And you let him live here in the house instead of bunking in with the other hands.'

'He has every right. He's your brother's child.'

'As if you'd let me forget.'

'I don't understand you, sometimes. You seem to begrudge the time we spent going to the aid of a young man who put himself in mortal danger to rescue our daughter. It's only luck that it's the kidnapper who was killed. It could just as easily have been Ryan.'

'Well, it wasn't, was it?' he snapped.

'Now why do I think you sound disappointed?' Val followed him into the office and positioned herself in front of him, leaning back on his desk and blocking his view of the computer. 'I think you know a lot more about this than you're saying. And there's one thing that's been puzzling me for some time. How did you know the kidnapper's name was Harry?'

His eyes widened and she saw the question had shocked him. 'I dunno.' He looked away, avoiding her penetrating gaze. 'Somebody must've — '

'No, they didn't. Nobody mentioned his name until you did. I remember it clearly. You said 'Ryan shot Harry.'' And she folded her arms, relishing the fact that she was making him squirm. 'I'd say you've known this man for some time and had dealings with him before — '

'Will you leave it, woman? I don't have time to listen to your scatty theories.'

'Then why are you getting upset? What am I saying that makes you so uncomfortable? You knew exactly how dangerous that man could be but you let Ryan go after him anyway, knowing full well that he might be killed.'

Robert had gone very red in the face. Panting, he leaned forward, clutching his chest. 'Quick, Val. Get me a drink of water. I think I'm having a heart attack,' he croaked.

'Water won't help if you are.' Val was unmoved, quick to see this was an attempt to divert her. 'I knew you were hiding something when you made up that cock-and-bull story about buying drugs for the horses. Did you really think I'd be fool enough to believe it?'

'OK. I admit it was stupid but I needed time to think.'

'What for? To invent a more plausible lie? But never mind that now. I want you to tell me about Harry Green — the hired killer at the centre of this, tale.' She went on before he could interrupt, 'And don't bother to lie because you're no good at hiding your feelings. I've been watching you, Rob, and when you heard the kidnapper had been shot, you weren't just relieved, you were almost elated.' She paused for a moment, allowing her words to sink in. 'Because it meant there was nobody left to point the finger at you.'

'Christ, woman, you have a good imagination. You should write a book.'

She continued, ignoring his feeble attempt to laugh it off. 'So — back to Harry Green. Who did you want him to kill and how did it all go so wrong?'

'I dunno what you mean.'

'I won't be fobbed off. Not this time. We've been married a long time, Rob, and nobody knows you better than I do. No one can hold a grudge longer than you and I think this resentment of yours is long-term, going all the way back to Joanne and Peter. They went as far away as they could to get away from you but it wasn't far enough. You still couldn't draw a line and leave them in peace.'

'I'd have left them in peace.' He shrugged, looking sullen. 'It was Peter who stirred things up. He took that beautiful, big grey horse that was earmarked for me.'

'That's not so. Hunter's Moon was up for sale to the highest bidder. And that person turned out not to be you.'

'No. It was bloody Peter again, standing in my light. Somehow he's always there, isn't he? Depriving me of whatever I want the most.'

'Including Joanne, I suppose.' Val sighed. 'Poor old Rob. Did you really love her that much?'

'Is that what you think?' He laughed shortly. 'No. I had a lucky escape there. You wouldn't have recognized her as I saw her last — aged before her time, twisted with grief.'

'Don't be cruel, Rob. The poor woman's dead.'

He made a dismissive gesture. 'Ah, she was a loser just like my brother. Why should I care about them?'

'You cared, all right. You cared enough to

drive halfway across the country to Peter's funeral. I thought it was odd at the time. But the funeral was just an excuse, wasn't it? Come hell or high water, you had to have that horse.'

'And I got him, didn't I? Give it a rest, Val.'

'I'll give it a rest when I get to the bottom of it. You still haven't told me why you needed Harry Green. And why you didn't pay him when the job was done. You must have known a man like that wouldn't take it lying down.'

'Christ, woman, you're like a terrier worrying a bone,' Rob snarled, all pretence of good temper gone. 'Let it alone, I say. Or you won't like what you hear.'

'I've lived with disappointment for most of our married life. There's not much you can say that would hurt me now.' She sighed yet again. 'After all, it isn't as if you ever loved me.'

'Love!' he said, mocking her. 'Does anyone really know what that is? It was a marriage of convenience for both of us as you very well know. It was common knowledge that your father was terminally ill and you, as his only heir, would inherit the lot. And you were in a tight enough corner yourself, expecting a child out of wedlock.'

'Yes. Thanks to you.'

'I've always wondered about that girl. I see

little of myself in her. And when you had that affair with the bloke from England, I started to wonder just how long it had been going on.'

'D'you honestly think he'd have gone back to England without me if Chrissie were his? She's yours, Robert, like it or not, although there have been times when I wish she wasn't.'

'Oho, now the truth is coming out. I was a fool, wasn't I? I thought if you had one child already, you'd be able to give me a son. But you couldn't even do that for me, could you?'

'God knows, Robert, I tried.' She straightened her shoulders and folded her arms. 'But you're dodging the issue as usual. I want to know about Harry Green and why you needed to hire such a dangerous man. Your resentment against Peter and his family has had a long time to fester. Or why would you be so upset when I brought the lad here?'

'I'm warning you, woman. Let it go. You're not going to like what you find.'

'I can't. Not now I'm getting so close. It all started with Hunter's Moon. I know how much you hate to lose and you lost the race you expected to give you the means to buy him. Then, to add insult to injury, you had to stand there and watch your despised younger brother pay over the odds to defeat you.'

'That horse is a champion. He'd never have reached his potential with Peter. They would have been racing him in the sticks against country nags.'

'While they were training him, yes. But Peter had much more ambition than you give him credit for. Didn't he bring a mare to Sydney to win an important race? That's how he made enough money to buy Hunter's Moon.'

'The horse that was meant to be mine.'

'But you couldn't just accept it and walk away. Oh, no. You had to give fate a little push. You couldn't wait to take a horsebox onto the highway, the moment you heard your brother was dead.' Her eyes widened as she realized she had stumbled on a very unpleasant truth. 'That's the connection, isn't it? Please don't tell me you hired that man to kill Peter in revenge for taking the horse?'

'Listen to yourself. What kind of monster d'you think I am?'

'A very vengeful one.'

'Peter's death was an accident. Everyone says so, including the girl who was on the beach with him. The coroner's verdict was quite clear: accidental death.'

'Coroners like tidy conclusions with no loose ends. It's all too easy to turn in a verdict of accidental death — case closed.'

'Let it go, Val. You're looking for sinister motives where there are none.'

'Am I? And what about Tony Raymond? Chrissie saw him that very day at the races less than an hour before he was knocked down in the street. Are you trying to tell me his death was an accident, too?'

'Of course it was!' Robert was finally losing his temper and yelling. 'All right — if you must know, I'll tell you! Harry made a mistake and killed the wrong guy. And that's the reason I wouldn't pay.'

Realizing he'd already said too much, he tried to push himself backwards to get away from her. Val was staring at him, horrified by this latest confession. 'Now you know everything. I hope you're satisfied. Not that you can do much about it. It's all speculation, anyway. And a wife can't give evidence against her husband, can she? I think that rule still applies.'

Val was speechless for a moment, struggling to come to terms with what she'd just heard. 'You hired that man to kill Ryan and make it look like an accident?' she whispered. 'Then he made a mistake and killed Tony instead.'

'There you have it.' Robert applauded softly. 'Doesn't matter. Tony Raymond's no loss to the world.'

'Only to his mother,' Val said. 'And it was the killer I saw that day at the hospital, wasn't it? When I came to collect you from rehab. You said he was just another patient, passing the time of day — but I thought it was odd at the time. You both seemed so intense and it preyed on my mind.'

'Well, it's too late to worry about that now. Pete's gone, Joanne's gone and now Harry's dead, too. No one left to punish, is there?'

'Only you.'

'Really? I'm in jail already; a poor old cripple in a wheelchair.'

Val sighed. 'But Robert, so many people have died and what for? So you could scramble over their bodies to get Hunter's Moon.' And she shivered, suddenly chilled.

Robert's eyes glittered. 'It'll be worth it, you'll see. I'll make a champion of him yet.'

Val folded her arms and smiled, shaking her head. 'But after all your plotting and planning, Tommy still isn't yours. Oh, he's physically here in your stables and you think you own him but really he doesn't belong to you. He's bonded with Ryan, Peter's son.'

'Sentimental nonsense!' Robert was speaking through clenched teeth. 'That animal's only as good as the prize money he can win and he hasn't won anything for me yet. D'you honestly think I care if he likes me or not?'

He started rummaging in a side drawer in his desk and Val realized he was searching for the revolver he kept there. He picked it up and checked it quickly to make sure it was loaded. 'I'll show you who's in charge here. I'll go down to the stables right now and put a bullet between his eyes.'

'And what good will that do?' Val felt the first stirring of panic, realizing she had said too much and pushed him too far. 'You won't have your champion then and you'll break Ryan's heart.'

'An added bonus.' Robert's face was a mask of fury, his smile a grimace. Anger provided him with speed as he turned the wheelchair and started moving towards the lift. Val hurried after him, grabbing the back of the chair and fighting to move it aside as her husband twisted around, threatening her with the gun. She knocked it out of his hand before he could fire it and it spun away across the polished floor. But their struggle caused the chair to spin away from her in another direction, flying backwards towards the wide flight of stairs. She lunged forward, trying to catch it, and missed, falling heavily on her knees.

Realizing his plight, Robert screamed. He felt for the brake but panic was making him fumble. The chair was gathering momentum and couldn't be stopped as it continued its backwards journey towards the stairs. With its helpless occupant still aboard, it bounced down the first flight before tossing him out when it reached the landing halfway. He rolled the rest of the way down to the hall, unable to stop. Val got unsteadily to her feet and looked over the bannister to see what had happened to him. He was lying motionless on the floor, the broken chair beside him, one wheel still spinning. It was impossible to tell if he was dead or alive.

She had to think quickly. Questions would be asked if a loaded revolver were to be found at the scene, so she seized it and wiped it off on her cardigan before returning it to its usual place in his desk. Fortunately, it hadn't been fired. The vacuum cleaner had long since ceased its roar and she knew Margie would have heard the commotion and come to see what had happened.

She did. Hands to her mouth, she stared at Robert, lying there motionless, and then up at Val, looking down on them from the floor above.

'I heard raised voices and then a scream,' Margie said. 'What happened, Val? Are you all right?'

'Robert lost control of his chair and fell down the stairs. D'you think he's dead?'

'I don't know,' Margie said. 'He's not moving but I don't want to touch him.' She shuddered.

'We should call an ambulance.'

'Yeah,' Margie said. 'You've gone awfully white, Val. Are you sure you're OK?'

'That's a stupid question.'

'Sorry.'

'No. It's not your fault, Margie, it's me.' Val closed her eyes briefly. 'I think I'm in shock. You should have heard the terrible things he said — '

'I did. Most of it, anyway. I didn't mean to but he was shouting so loud, I couldn't avoid it. I've always felt sorry for you — married to him. He wasn't a nice man.'

'You're speaking as if he's already dead.'

'One can hope.' Margie smiled grimly, holding up her hand for silence. She was dialling triple 0.

'Yeah, it's the boss,' she said after giving the details. 'Seems to be unconscious — probably dead.' She listened for a moment more before hanging up. 'Ambulance is on its way,' she said.

On legs that were shaking so much she could hardly control them, Val came downstairs to look at her husband. He didn't appear to be breathing and she knew she should attempt some form of resuscitation, but she couldn't bring herself to do so after that confession and all the horrible things he'd said. Wasn't it better to let fate decide?

'Should we get him a pillow or something?' Margie said, breaking into her thoughts. 'I don't know anything about first aid.'

'I've heard that moving a person can do more harm than good. Better wait for the experts. But you might fetch a blanket to keep him warm.'

'OK,' Margie said, oddly unmoved by the tragedy. 'Then I could make us some tea while we're waiting. I'm sure you can do with it.'

Hot, sweet tea was made and they sipped it in silence because there was really nothing to say. From time to time they took a peek at Robert, who still hadn't moved.

It was a good twenty minutes before the paramedics arrived.

'So sorry.' The senior man hurried in, followed by his assistant. 'But there's never enough of us to go round. Too many urgent calls at the same time.' He knelt to make a quick examination of Robert before replacing the blanket, covering his face this time.

'Nothing we could have done for this one, anyway. Neck's broken an' I think his back may be, too. Must've been one hell of a fall,' he said, glancing at the stairs. 'We better inform the cops.' Ryan and Chrissie arrived just as the ambulance was leaving. There were several police cars in the driveway and the house was a blaze of lights.

'Oh, God, what is it?' Chrissie said. 'I hope nothing's happened to Mum.'

Her relief was so obvious when she heard it was Robert who was on his way to the morgue and not Val, that the police exchanged significant glances. Unfortunately, the officer in charge was Inspector Ian Jackson who had been at school with Robert and had known him for some years. From the way he was looking at Ryan through narrowed eyes, Chrissie was grateful that her cousin had a cast-iron alibi and couldn't be suspected of having anything to do with her father's demise.

All the same, the inspector's investigation was thorough and he grilled Margie for a long time concerning Val and her attitude towards her husband. Were they a loving couple or did she hear them quarrelling? Was Val always patient with her invalid husband? It was clear that he wanted Margie to tell him the marriage was less than perfect. Margie shrugged, professing ignorance. 'I just work here,' she said, dismissing his theories. 'Not my place to wonder if they're happy or not.'

His sergeant meanwhile was measuring various distances from the lift to the stairs and from Robert's office. Val had no idea what they were expecting to find. It didn't help that Inspector Jackson had heard of the recent kidnapping, which only seemed to deepen his suspicions. In the end, it was some time before he could be satisfied that neither Val nor Margie had contributed to Robert's death. He left, promising to see them all at the coroner's inquest, and warning them all not to leave this present address until that was over.

# 15

At the coroner's inquest on Robert Lanigan's death, both Val and Margie had given their accounts of what happened and had gone to the back of the room to sit with Ryan and Chrissie. Everything seemed to be going smoothly enough until Inspector Jackson took the stand.

'The deceased was lying on the floor in the hall at the foot of the stairs with his broken wheelchair beside him,' he said, reading from his notes in a monotone. 'I knew Mr Lanigan personally and it seems odd that such an accident could happen to a man familiar with the dangers of his upstairs environment. But we have no reason to suppose it was anything other than an unfortunate accident. Mr Lanigan had been confined to a wheelchair since the vehicle he was driving collided with a truck in New South Wales but, in spite of his condition, he didn't seem unduly depressed. His wife mentioned that he was in reasonable spirits as he expected eventually to regain the use of his legs. She hadn't told him his doctors considered this unlikely. We have no reason to think he committed suicide by deliberately backing his chair to the stairwell or,' he paused to look at Val, 'any solid evidence to suppose that anyone pushed him.'

'Thank you, Inspector.' The coroner glanced at his watch. It was well after midday and his stomach was growling, reminding him that he needed lunch.

'However,' the inspector continued, raising his voice and earning himself a sigh from the coroner. 'In the course of my investigation I saw little evidence that Mr Lanigan was going to be mourned or missed. Throughout all our conversations, Mrs Lanigan and her daughter remained dry-eyed. So I have to say this led me to wonder — '

'We are not paid to wonder, Inspector.' The coroner fixed him with a stern look. 'We are here to deal with only the facts. And if you have no more facts to lay before us . . . ?'

'I don't have any more facts. No. It's just a feeling I have — ' The inspector had clearly hoped for a more sympathetic audience.

'In the face of no further solid evidence, I must return a verdict of accidental death.' And scarcely waiting for the formalities to be completed, the coroner banged his gavel and hurried from the room in search of lunch.

'We're lucky the old boy was starving, Mum.' Chrissie watched him leave, hastening down the steps at the front of the courthouse.

'I think Inspector Jackson was hoping to pin something on you.'

'I'm just tired of the whole sorry business, Chrissie.' Val sighed. 'As I said at the inquest, I tried to catch the chair but, if I had, I wouldn't be here to tell the tale. He was a heavy man and I would have been dragged down the stairs with him. But at least the inquest is over. Now we can arrange the funeral and get on with our lives.'

'You do realize that Hunter's Moon and the stables belong to you, Mum. Now you can do whatever you like and you don't have to answer to anyone.' She glanced at her telephone and saw there was a message from Sir Henry Wheeler, asking her to call him. 'I wonder what's up?' she said with an anxious glance at Ryan. 'I hope nothing's wrong.'

'Well, call him,' Val said, 'and find out.'

'I have good news, Chrissie,' the old man said when she contacted him. 'Walker and Associates, your ex-employers, have pushed too many people too far. There's to be a class action against them for several wrongful dismissals and I'm wondering whether you'd care to join them to help build a stronger case?'

'Oh, Uncle Henry, I don't think so,' she said. 'I want nothing more to do with those people, let alone work for them again.'

'No, my darling, you don't understand. This isn't about getting your old job back — it's about compensation and retrieving your good name.'

'I don't care about the compensation.'

'Then you should. Some of these young people don't have wealthy families to fall back on. We feel certain the Walkers will want to avoid the publicity and settle out of court. So how do you feel about it now?'

'Thank you, Uncle Henry. I was being selfish. Of course I'll join in. I'd very much like to get rid of this black mark against me.'

'I only wish you'd mentioned it to me before. We could have started something sooner. These people have been taking advantage of promising young graduates for too long.'

'I didn't think about it. I thought it was only me.'

'That's what everyone thought — until some of them started comparing notes. I'll keep you posted, Chrissie.'

*　*　*

Robert's funeral was surprisingly well-attended. Although he wasn't a popular figure at the track, arrogant and irascible towards those he considered his rivals and far from generous towards reporters, maybe most people were there to make sure he was really dead. Val and Chrissie were formally dressed in black and Sir Henry was with them, lending respectability and old-world charm.

The service was conducted in a chapel attached to the crematorium, the venue hastily changed to a larger room as more people than expected kept arriving to pay their respects. The minister who conducted the service had no personal knowledge of Robert and could offer little more than the standard platitudes. The coffin, after the conventional display of white lilies had been removed, disappeared into the inferno that could be heard roaring behind the curtains in record time. Shortly afterwards, Val and Chrissie found themselves outside, receiving condolences and examining a multitude of floral tributes from people they scarcely knew.

Most people don't attend weddings unless they're invited but that wasn't the case with this funeral as Val quickly found out. A lot more people than she was expecting descended on her house like a swarm of locusts, expecting to be fed. Luckily, Margie's sister was in catering and was persuaded to come to the rescue with a van full of sandwiches and snacks. Robert's precious hoard of single-malt whisky was raided to provide bracing drinks for everyone and, after a while, people forgot that it was a funeral feast and turned it into a party. All that was missing was music and dancing. It was well into the evening before everyone left and went home. Margie was last to leave, telling Val and Chrissie to leave the room as it was and get some rest; she would be back to clear up first thing in the morning.

'The worst is over now, Mum,' Chrissie said, hugging her mother, who seemed slighter than usual, these days. 'But you look exhausted. You need to sleep.'

Val headed for the stairs, too tired even to reply.

'I'll go and check on Tommy before I turn in,' Ryan said. 'I haven't seen him all day.'

'I'll come with you,' Chrissie said, catching his hand and linking her fingers with his.

Tommy was pleased to see Ryan as always, no matter what time of the day or night it might be, although he regarded Chrissie with suspicion and stamped his foot when Ryan put a protective arm around her.

'You don't have to be jealous, old chap,' Ryan said, rubbing the colt's nose. 'We'll have you covering all the mares you can handle, when the time comes.'

Chrissie broke free, laughing. 'I'm not sure I like being called a mare to be handled,' she said.

'Ssh.' Ryan knew she was teasing. 'I have to

put it in terms that Tommy will understand.'

They wandered through the stables and Chrissie was surprised to see so many unusually clean and empty stalls with tack hanging unused on the walls.

'I knew Dad had lost a few horses,' she said. 'But nobody told me it was as bad as this.'

'Look on the bright side,' Ryan said. 'Your father wasn't the easiest man to get along with — '

'You can say that again,' Chrissie said with a wry smile.

'And when Tommy attracts new owners to the stables — as he will — they'll be people who've chosen us because they have faith in your mother — and ourselves.' He pulled her into his arms and he rested his chin on her head. 'What is that? You smell wonderful.'

'Stick to the point.'

'Chrissie, there's something I haven't told you. Very soon I must go back up north.'

She drew back and looked up into his face, wide-eyed. 'No, Ryan. Why?'

'Don't look so stricken. It won't be for long. Just long enough to make a deal with Glen Harrison about the old farm.'

'You've decided to sell it, then?'

'I could probably manage it long distance without going up there at all, but Glen's a businessman first and he might be tempted to cheat me. He'll offer me a far better price if I'm there on the spot twisting his arm.'

'I could go with you. I've never been up north.'

'Another time. You need to be here, helping your uncle with the case against the Walkers. And it won't be for long — I'll get my dad's old solicitors to handle it soon as we've agreed on a price.'

She reached up to place her arms around his neck and raised her face to be kissed. Willingly, he obliged.

'You'll sleep in my room tonight, Ryan,' she whispered.

'Whoa.' He opened his eyes to look at her. 'What about your . . . ?'

'Mum will sleep forever. She's exhausted. I'll go in first and you come up in about half an hour.'

He caught her in yet another embrace before she could leave. 'Oh, Chrissie, I love you so much.'

'I know. And I love you too,' she said with an impish smile.

★   ★   ★

Inside the house, Chrissie listened at her mother's door, rewarded by the sound of gentle snoring. She wasn't at all sure her mother would understand or approve of the relationship she was conducting with her cousin but right now she didn't care. She wanted Ryan in a way that she'd never wanted anyone in her whole life and she was prepared to make herself the centre of his. And she knew, without a doubt, that he felt the same. He was straightforward and uncomplicated, carrying no baggage from previous affairs. On reaching her bedroom, she leaned back against the door and closed her eyes, overcome by a wave of desire, imagining Ryan's strong, young body hard against her own. She hoped he wouldn't be long.

He wasn't. She had time only to have a quick shower, anoint herself with her favourite Jo Malone body crème, put on her newest silk nightgown and turn down all the lights before he was there. He came in stealthily, without knocking, and just as she had done, leaned back for a moment against the door.

'Oh,' he whispered. 'It smells lovely in here. Is it you or the room?'

'Come here,' she said, sensing his diffidence as she took him by the hand and led him to the bed. She pushed him down onto it and straddled him, unembarrassed by her own forwardness.

'Chrissie,' he said, suddenly anxious. 'I

don't want to disappoint you but I don't — that is, I haven't — '

'Been with a girl before.' She smiled down at him. 'Don't worry. I'm not all that experienced myself. We'll just do what seems right and let nature take its course.'

Nature did. Clumsy and over-anxious at first, they were able to make love many times, becoming attuned to each other's needs and marvelling at the pleasure they could give and receive. Caught up in the excitement of new love, soon the rest of the world ceased to exist for them and they lost all sense of time. At last, sated and locked in each other's arms, they fell into a dreamless and exhausted sleep. They heard nothing until there was a soft knocking at the door in the morning, bringing them instantly awake as if a bucket of cold water had been thrown over them.

Ryan dived under the covers and Chrissie covered his head with her spare pillow, pushing the bedclothes around him in the hope that her mother wouldn't see anything more than a dishevelled bed.

'Good morning.' Val almost sang the words. She had recovered from the ordeal of attending Robert's funeral and seemed like her old self again. She placed a tray with two cups of coffee and two croissants with jam and butter on the table beside the bed. 'It's all right, Ryan, I know you're in there. Breakfast is served and you can come out now.'

Sheepishly, Ryan sat up, revealing a tousled head.

'Are you all right with this, Mum?' Chrissie said. 'You're not upset?'

'Bit late to worry about that now, isn't it?' Val sat down on the bed. 'I'm a child of the swinging sixties, remember — not that easy to shock. I went to sleep much too early and found myself wide awake in the early hours. So I went down to the stables to look at the records and think about starting a campaign to bring us new owners. When Ryan didn't turn up to look after Tommy as usual, I asked Jim to feed the colt and came back to the house to rouse him, only to find an empty bed. And, as you two have been so close lately, it was a small step to conclude that he must be in yours.'

'You don't have to worry, Mum.' Chrissie sighed. 'It's only a one-night stand — we know it can't happen again. We are in love, yes.' She took Ryan's hand and held it close as if to give herself strength to say it. 'But we both know nothing can come of it because we're too closely related.'

'But that's what I'm here to tell you, my darling. You're not.'

She had their full attention then; they were both instantly wide awake.

'So what are you saying?' Chrissie whispered. 'That the conniving old bastard you married wasn't really my father?'

'Oh, come on, that's a bit strong, even for you,' Val smiled. 'I hope you're not worried about speaking ill of the dead?'

'Not in his case. A man who can employ a commando to do all his dirty work because he can't find the courage to do it himself.'

'I get the point. Don't say any more.' Val placed a hand on her shoulder to calm her. 'Sorry to raise your hopes only to dash them but Rob Lanigan really was your father. The difference comes from Ryan's side of the family.'

Ryan spoke for the first time. 'Oh no, Val, you have to be wrong about that. My mother would never have been unfaithful. She never loved anyone but Peter, my father.'

'I know. They were the romance of the century. But nobody ever told you — or Peter for that matter — that he himself was adopted as a baby.'

'I don't think so. That would have come out before now. Anyway, how can you be so sure?'

'Because I heard it from Claire Lanigan herself, the boys' mother. It's a heartbreaking story. She felt as though her whole life was blighted because her sons couldn't be friends.' She paused to pass each of them a cup of coffee and a croissant. 'Eat your breakfast while it's warm and I'll tell you what I know. Claire told me only because I pressed her. As I was marrying Robert, I wanted to know everything about him, including the cause of his animosity towards his younger brother that seemed to be there even before he married Joanne.

'Your grandparents married late in life and, after Robert was born, Claire was told there would be no more children. Not wanting Robert to grow up alone, she persuaded her husband to let her adopt another baby boy when their son was just eighteen months old. She went away for a month or so before the adoption and when she returned, she let friends and relatives assume the child was her own. She visualized her boys growing up with a strong bond between them; two young men standing together against the world. But it didn't turn out that way. Robert was jealous of the baby and loathed him almost at first sight. Claire kept hoping he'd get over it and the boys would be friends, but instead the situation went from bad to worse. Nor did it help that her husband loved Peter more than his natural son and didn't trouble to hide his feelings. Robert reminded him too much of his own father, who had been a stern disciplinarian and believed in regular beatings to 'form character' or so he said.

'More comparisons were made as the boys grew older. Peter was a natural horseman, in tune with his father's lifestyle, while Robert was always too stiff and heavy to sit well on a horse. And in later life, when they were both adults, Robert had to watch Joanne reject him in favour of the younger brother he detested. Their father died unexpectedly, leaving the stables to both of them, but Robert wouldn't rest until he had sole ownership, driving Peter away. Claire never found the courage to tell either of them the truth about Peter's adoption and she died, leaving the burden of that knowledge with me. At the time, I thought the secret might as well stay buried with Claire. Since Peter and Joanne were building a new life together up north, I thought there was no need to tell as our paths would never cross. Until the cyclone came and turned the whole world upside down.'

'Wait a moment, Mum,' Chrissie said. 'How can you be sure that this is really the truth? I remember Nan Lanigan and she was a strange old bird. How do you know she didn't make it all up?'

'Here comes the lawyer, wanting proof as

usual.' Val smiled. 'Claire Lanigan had a secret compartment in her old Victorian desk and she showed it to me. That's where she kept the adoption papers. She made me promise that if anything happened to her, I would go and clear her desk before Robert found them. He was hopping mad when he discovered the secret compartment with nothing inside it. He'd been so certain it would contain money or jewels.'

'Can I see those papers, if you still have them?' Ryan said softly. 'I'd like to see the proof of who I really am.'

'Of course,' Val said. 'They belong to you now that Peter's gone.'

'Oh, Mum,' Chrissie said, clasping her mother's hand. 'Thank you so much for this news. You don't know what this means to us.'

'Well, I couldn't let you go on agonizing, thinking you were doing something wrong.' Val smiled. 'It's all right. In today's world, relationships can be much more casual. So if this is no more than a little adventure — a one-night stand — no one will think any the worse of you for it.'

'Make no mistake, Val,' Ryan said. 'This isn't a trivial thing to me at all. I love Chrissie. Really, I do. But it's still early days for us. And if she doesn't want to marry, that's OK with me, too.'

267

'We're not related,' Chrissie hugged him. 'I feel as if I've had the best Christmas and birthday present all rolled into one.'

# 16

As Tommy was having a rest in the paddock before getting down to the serious business of the Spring Carnival, Ryan took a short break to go back to Canesville for the first time since he left many months before. He didn't want to put added pressure on Chrissie after all she'd been through nor did he want her to think he was too needy. If he was honest with himself, he was passionately in love and wanted to spend the rest of his life with her. But somehow he knew that this was the time to give her some space.

Glen Harrison himself met him at the airport in Cairns and, as they drove north, Ryan could see that many changes had already been made. Wherever possible and there was money enough to spend, old or damaged buildings were being replaced by new ones and, as plants grow fast and healing happens quickly in the tropics, he could see that many farmers had optimistically planted their crops again and his old home town was well on the way to recovery.

As they turned down the narrow lane that led to his parents' property, Ryan's throat tightened and he felt close to tears as Glen chattered on of plans to remake and widen the road, unaware of his young companion's emotional turmoil. Back in these familiar surroundings, the events of the past came all too vividly to life. Ryan could almost hear his father's voice in his head, grooming him to be his successor and helping him to understand the business of training horses. There was also the clean, fresh smell of a tropical sea that had been absent from his life for too long, reminding him of the joys of galloping along a beach. He could bear to think of it only now he knew his father's death was no accident and hadn't been caused by his beloved horse.

When they came to a full stop outside the ruins of his old home, Ryan had to fight for composure. The tree that had killed his mother was still lying where it had fallen; no one had troubled to move it or cut it up. The old homestead itself was water-damaged from the heavy rains that had followed the cyclone, but Ryan, seeing it now through a visitor's eyes, thought it seemed a lot smaller and poorer than the home he remembered.

He cleared his throat when he was at last able to speak. 'Mum was right,' he said. 'If the roof had been mended and strengthened, we might have got away with it and the house would still have been standing.'

'I doubt it, Ryan. Like so many of these old weatherboard homes, it was old and coming to the end of its useful life. But your father was wise to add a new stable block — that will give a buyer something to think about. And when we've built something more solid to replace your old home and put in a swimming pool, along with some other amenities — '

'I'm sorry, Glen,' Ryan broke in, close to tears again. 'I thought I could do this but I can't. Coming here has brought back too many memories. I don't want to go inside to see if there's anything left — '

'There won't be,' Glen muttered. 'Soon as the roads were open again, looters came in from everywhere; vultures picking over the ruins. They seemed to know when a place had been abandoned.' He paused for a moment, giving the younger man time to take in what he had seen and collect his thoughts. 'So what is your thinking now, Ryan? Are you willing to sell to me now? Or do you still need more time?'

'There's no point in further delay. I'll never live here again,' Ryan said, forgetting all about his boasts to Chrissie of driving a hard bargain. 'Even visiting here has been a mistake.' He looked at the stable block, thinking of Sprite, who would no longer whinny a greeting from the doorway of her stall. 'I wish I'd never come.'

'No.' Glen wasn't unsympathetic. 'I think you needed to come back and see the old place as it is today. Only then can you move on.'

'I'm sure you're right.' He lowered his head to hide the tears as he turned back towards Glen's car. He had seen enough.

'Come on, we'll get over to my place and look at the paperwork. I don't know if you drink, Ryan, but you look as if you could use one.'

Back at the Harrison home, Ryan started to feel better. Glen's smooth-running, polished environment was just as he remembered and somehow comforting — especially without the abrasive presence of Fiona. As if reading his thoughts, Glen mentioned her.

'I have to thank you, Ryan, for opening my eyes and helping me to get out of that woman's clutches. Believe me when I say it'll be a long time before I let another one get that close. You can tell that to Mike when you see him; he never liked Fiona.'

Ryan flushed and looked away.

'Oh no,' Glen said. 'What's he done this time? You used to be the one friend he didn't alienate.'

'Honestly, it's nothing.'

'I think it is. Or you wouldn't look so uncomfortable.'

'All right. He tried to hit on my cousin and I didn't like it because I — '

'I get it. Mike was up to his old tricks, trying to muscle in on your girl?'

'It didn't matter before. Mike has always been better-looking than I am. I never used to care that he got all the girls.'

'Until you found this one. I do hope he didn't succeed?'

'No.' Ryan laughed shortly. 'And that didn't suit him, either.'

'It'll do Mike good to get one or two knock-backs. He doesn't appreciate girls because he can get them so easily. My fault too, I suppose. Letting him run around in sports cars as soon as he could drive.' Glen paused to take a gulp of whisky. Ryan had scarcely touched the one poured for him. 'Make no mistake, I'm proud of my son, Ryan. Most people see just the playboy, but he's working hard now he's studying medicine. Doing well, too. Eventually, he'll make a brilliant surgeon.'

'Yes, I know.'

'Make it up with him, if you can. I know how shallow and flippant he can be but you mean a lot to him, really. I wouldn't like to see him lose you.'

273

Ryan nodded but he was making no promises.

'And now let us get down to business.' Glen clapped his hands, shifting quickly from concerned father to super salesman. 'I've done my researches and I know what your property's worth.'

'Good. Because I don't. And I suppose you'll think I'm stupid to be that honest.'

'No. I respect you for it. And because you saved me a lot of money by opening my eyes to that parasite, Fiona, I'm prepared to pay well over the market price. My solicitors have drawn up the contracts and as there's no mortgage or finance broker involved, we don't have to wait.' And he opened the briefcase by his chair and pushed the contracts over to Ryan. 'I don't expect you to sign today. Take them to your father's solicitors and let them confirm what I say.'

Ryan's eyes widened when he saw the amount. 'It seems like a lot of money for our poor, broken house.'

'I wouldn't be offering it, if I didn't think I could make more. I'm hoping to get planning permission for a luxury guest house. That's why I want to widen the road and open the access. It'll make all the difference.'

Ryan did drink the whisky now and it made him cough.

Later when he saw his father's solicitors, they advised him to take the offer and sign immediately. Glen Harrison didn't usually have the reputation of being so generous.

★　★　★

Ryan returned to Melbourne with more money in the bank than he had seen in the whole of his life. His mind was whirling with plans of what could be done with it and he couldn't wait to discuss them with Chrissie. He knew he couldn't be truly happy unless he could marry her but was that really what she wanted, too? When Val had discovered them in bed together, there had been flippant talk of casual relationships and one-night stands so what did Chrissie really want? Would the spark of passion that had grown up between them die a natural death when it was no longer forbidden fruit? He couldn't make any more plans for the future until he found out. They needed to sit down and have a serious talk.

As arranged before, Chrissie met him at Tullamarine Airport and he thought she looked tired and a little strained. She greeted him with a kiss that was warm as ever but behind it, he was sensing a new reserve. So what was the matter now?

'I'm happy for you,' she said when she heard how smoothly the sale had gone and the generous sum now sitting in his bank account. 'You'll have enough money to get your own place now. If that's what you want.'

'And is that what you want me to do?' he asked. Unreasonably, he felt a frisson of anger towards her. Obviously, she couldn't wait to push him away. 'Chrissie, we can't talk about serious stuff like this while you're driving. We need to stop for a coffee and thrash this out.'

'We're always doing this, Ryan. Stopping in the middle of some journey.'

'I don't care. We need to have a serious talk and we can't do that in a car — we'll end up wrapping it around a tree.'

'We'd be together for all time then, wouldn't we?' She considered the thought. 'I wonder if there is an eternity?'

'You're in a strange mood today, Chrissie. Not like yourself at all. Why?'

She sighed. 'You're quite right. We do need to talk without Mum listening in. We should do it before we get home.'

His heart sank as he sensed an ominous meaning behind her words. She didn't sound at all like a woman in love.

They found a roadside café and sat at the far end of it, which was deserted, so that other people wouldn't hear what they had to say. Ryan wanted to shake the story out of her immediately but he waited until there was a mug of strong coffee in front of both of them. He leaned forward, trying to read the expression on her face, which was carefully blank and telling him nothing. She pulled a face at the coffee, not really wanting to drink it.

'Right,' he said. 'Whatever's the matter, give it to me straight. As I see it, we should be leaping for joy, throwing our caps in the air. We're not even half related. I have more money than I've ever seen in my life and we're in love. Don't you like being happy? Because what can possibly be the matter now?'

She astonished him by bursting into tears. Not knowing what else to do, he went and gathered a pile of napkins from a dispenser, handed them to her silently and waited for her to get over this storm of weeping. One or two people glared at him, thinking he must have upset her.

'Chrissie, what's wrong?' he said at last. 'This isn't like you at all. You're usually so amazingly brave. Has something happened to your mother? Is she ill?'

The girl wept for a while longer, still unable to speak. Finally, she blew her nose noisily and took a deep breath. Then she looked up at him, trying to smile.

'No. Mum's fine. In fact she's more than fine. There was a man — someone from England that she was in love with once. She thought he was married but he's not. And he got in touch as soon as he heard my father was dead. He's flying over to see her — might even be on his way now.'

'But that's a good thing, isn't it? Aren't you happy for her?'

'Oh, yes. I'm not crying about that. It's me — I've been an emotional mess lately.' Tears welled in her eyes once more, making him reach out to take her hands to steady her. 'I'm so sorry, Ryan. I should have been more careful. But I'm pregnant.'

He stared at her for a moment, taking it in. This was the last thing he had expected.

She misinterpreted his astonished expression. 'No. It's all right, you don't have to worry. I'm not expecting you to marry me or anything. You're so young and you have your whole life ahead of you — '

'You have to stop harping on about how young I am. Why on earth did you think I wouldn't be pleased? Oh, Chrissie, this is wonderful news. A new life — a child of our own.'

'But it's too soon. You need to have fun — to — '

'To do what? Go to discos and dance with vapid girls? I've done all that already with Mike and it wasn't much fun, let me tell you.' He paused, struck by a thought that made him uneasy. 'You do want to keep the baby? You wouldn't be thinking of — of — '

'No way.' She understood him immediately. 'Oh Ryan, how could I have doubted you even for a moment?'

'We'll get married right away. There doesn't have to be a fuss. Just a quiet civil ceremony.'

'No one would expect anything else — not after what happened to Dad. Will Mike come and stand up as a witness for you?'

'I can only ask. His father wants me to make it up with him. But when I think how he left you alone in the street to be grabbed by those kidnappers — '

'They would have found another way to get at me if he hadn't. You can't hold Mike responsible.'

Ryan shrugged.

'Come on.' She smiled, almost herself again. 'Best friends aren't that easy to come by. You can ask Mike and I'll ask Michelle. Mum says she's back from her trip overseas. She's a little acid drop but I think you'll like her. She never liked Tony.'

'Oh, now I'm really worried. Supposing she doesn't like me?'

But Michelle did like him when they all met at a popular café in town. She had changed her appearance since Chrissie last saw her. The long blonde hair had been cut short and turned into boyish tufts that stood out all over her head, making her look younger than ever, like a cheeky Peter Pan.

'You lucky old thing,' she said, nudging Chrissie as they watched Ryan leave them to fight for more drinks at the bar. 'He's just gorgeous.'

'Oh, I don't know that he'd like that description,' Chrissie laughed.

'Well, he is. Chunky and there's just no other word for it — gorgeous. Don't you know that sandy-haired men are all the rage now? Taken over from the tall, dark and handsome. They say it's all because of Prince Harry. Your guy reminds me of Channing Tatum — did you see him in that film about male strippers?' Michelle's eyes sparkled. 'Oh yeah.'

Chrissie giggled. 'Michelle, that's enough! You do talk a lot of rot. And hands off. I saw him first.'

'Yeah, dammit,' Michelle teased before becoming serious. 'It's obvious that he adores you, Chrissie, and that's nice to see.'

'Oh, Michelle, you don't know how I've missed you. And you will come to our wedding, won't you? It's going to be very low-key.'

'Yes. Long as Ryan turns up with a best friend for me.'

'But his best friend is last year's model. The tall, dark and handsome variety. Medical student.'

'Wow! I can't wait.'

'But the package comes with a strong warning concerning reliability.'

'I don't need him to be reliable. He has to be more exciting than the dull accountant types I've been dating lately.'

Chrissie laughed. 'Mike Harrison may be many things but he certainly isn't dull.'

*   *   *

Walter Mannion wasn't dull either, although his appearance was a surprise to Chrissie when she and her mother went to meet him on his arrival at Tullamarine Airport. She thought Val would want to meet him alone, but her mother insisted that she should be there in case there was any awkwardness between them after all this time.

Val needn't have worried. Although it was many years since she had seen him, Walter seemed astonishingly unchanged and she could only hope he felt the same way about her. Well dressed in smart but casual clothes, he was a small, compact Englishman who had been a jockey before becoming a trainer and then turning his talents towards breeding horses. Before saying anything, he swept Val into a warm embrace as if he had seen her only yesterday and Chrissie was slightly bemused, watching her mother bloom under this man's obvious admiration. Walter wasn't a man who would ever take her for granted. In the end, Chrissie realized that, apart from acting as chauffeur, there had been absolutely no need for her to be there. Val and Walter sat together on the back seat, talking endlessly and holding each other's hands as if they would never let go.

'I have a confession to make,' he told Val at last.

'Oh no, Walter, don't spoil it. You really don't have to tell me anything.' Val was suddenly afraid this reunion was going to be all too good to be true.

'No,' he said. 'This is important. When I wrote to you when my wife died and you still wouldn't join me in England, I told a lie when I said I'd married again. At that point I could see that you'd never leave Robert so I wanted you to forget me — perhaps even hate me a little.'

'Oh, Walter, I could never hate you. You

must have known you'd always be there in my heart.'

'Can you forgive me?'

'Oh, my darling, you're here now. You came back to me. There's really nothing to forgive.'

Chrissie concentrated on the road, trying not to watch the two lovebirds as they clung together like teenagers. She could only wonder what was going to happen now. Walter clearly had no intention of parting from Val again; she was the love of his life. But his breeding stables and the whole of his operation was centred in England. They would have to sit down and thrash out a plan for the future if they wanted to be together.

Walter was impressed with the Lanigans' stables and ran a practised hand over Tommy as Ryan gave him a brief summary of the animal's history. He left nothing out, including the rivalry of the brothers who had fought so long and hard to possess him.

'But I guess he belongs to Val now,' he said at last. 'And it's up to her to decide what we do with him next.'

'If he wins his next race, he will qualify for the Melbourne Cup,' Val said. 'We can only hope there aren't too many overseas entries coming this year. The organizers are all too ready to overlook some of our local heroes in favour of visitors and that can be frustrating sometimes. Something to do with worldwide television coverage.'

'Well, let's hope he makes it.' Walter gave Tommy a final pat on the neck. 'He's certainly big and strong enough to be a good stayer.'

* * *

The dinner party of eight around the kitchen table that evening was the largest gathering there had been for some time, the reason being to discuss the upcoming plans for the wedding. As well as Val, Walter, Chrissie and Ryan, Mike Harrison and Michelle were also invited together with Margie and her husband, Ron, making up the party.

The registry office was considered and rejected as being too impersonal and then Margie put forward the suggestion that a less formal ceremony could take place outside on the lawn. She and her sister would be happy to cater the event as it was small.

'May I say something?' Walter spoke up at last. He had been unusually silent for quite a while.

'Please do.' Chrissie smiled at him, ready to listen to anyone who could make her mother this happy.

'I haven't asked Val about this so I really

have no idea what her answer will be,' he said softly. 'And I know it's not very long since your father died, Chrissie, but your mother and I have already lost a lot of time. We don't have to have a double wedding if nobody likes the idea but it would be wonderful if Val would marry me on the same day.' So saying, he put a small black velvet box in front of Val on the table. 'Please, my darling, say yes this time.' And he sat back and closed his eyes, half-expecting rejection again.

Val opened the box and everyone gasped at the size of the diamond inside, reflecting the candlelight nearby.

'Oh, Walter, I don't know. There's so much to think about,' she said, biting her lip.

'No, it's easy and simple,' he said. 'I know it's too soon and people will talk but you do want to marry me, don't you?'

'You know I do.'

'All right. Now this is the plan and I've been thinking about it a lot. Most of the time we'll live in England, finding and breeding good horses to send to your daughter and son-in-law here. Let them spread their wings and realize their potential, training and racing those horses on their own; I'm sure we can get Ryan a trainer's licence even if we have to pull a few strings. And when Hunter's Moon has done enough, we'll take him to England to incorporate him into our breeding programme there.'

'Oh no,' Ryan started to say. 'After all we've been through, I can't lose him.'

'You won't,' Walter said as if he'd been half-expecting this response. 'Because we're not going to be strangers here. The world is much smaller than it used to be. You'll visit us often just as we shall come here.' He paused for a moment, looking at Val. 'You've not answered me, Val. I do hope I haven't assumed too much? Please say you'll marry me?'

'Yes, Walter, yes.' Val could scarcely speak for the tears misting her eyes. 'How could I refuse?'

'Then let's celebrate and congratulate the happy couples.' Margie jumped up and went to raid the fridge. 'I had a feeling something like this might happen, so I put two nice bottles of French champagne to cool off in there.'

# 17

For once, Melbourne's unpredictable weather didn't let them down. Although it was still officially winter, the day dawned bright and clear with no clouds in the sky and no sign of rain. Margie and her friends had constructed a pretty arch of white roses at the end of a wisteria-covered walkway. Tinka, who had once been wary and frightened of strangers, ran around barking joyfully, having adapted well to this new environment of people and horses.

Both Chrissie and her mother wore simple dresses in a style reminiscent of the sixties. Val chose to wear a small cap made from the same fabric as her dress while Chrissie wore a small coronet of real flowers with other small, white flowers scattered throughout her abundant hair. Also, as the ceremony was informal and with no attendants, they decided not to carry flowers.

Michelle caught Mike's attention immediately but she received his overtures with a coolness that made Chrissie smile. This wasn't the same girl at all who had seemed so starry-eyed at the prospect of spending the day with him. If this was a strategy on her part, it was certainly working as he couldn't take his eyes off her; it would do Mike good to jump through hoops for once in his efforts to impress a girl.

The marriage celebrant, who looked as pretty as the two brides in a figure-hugging white suit, turned up in a chauffeur-driven white sports car. Moments after her arrival, the wedding ceremony was under way; the woman wanted to waste no time. With no music or singing, just a sincere exchange of the two couples' vows, it was over in minutes and the marriage celebrant climbed back into her car and was driven away to perform yet another ceremony that day. The rest of the wedding party headed back to the house for the celebrations to begin.

Ryan and Chrissie, anxious to seize a moment or two for themselves, lingered in the garden to savour the moment before joining the others. They had almost reached the front door when a small, black sedan came up the drive towards them, wheels spinning and spraying gravel as it was travelling too fast. Not recognizing the car, they both turned towards it, wondering who was about to gatecrash the party. It stopped with a squeal of brakes and the driver sprang out of the driver's seat to confront them.

Chrissie recognized him at once. It was Harry's son, Tim.

Shaking with rage or nerves, he staggered towards them and Chrissie's heart sank when she saw he was carrying a pistol, although he wasn't pointing it at anyone yet.

'S-so,' he said, shaking so much he could scarcely speak. 'The h-happy couple — '

Chrissie tried to take a step towards him but Ryan held her back.

'Oh, Timmy, why are you here? You don't want to ruin our wedding day.'

'I don't care. Why should you be happy when I'm not!' he raged at her. 'And don't call me Timmy! Only my mum ever called me that.'

'Chrissie,' Ryan whispered. 'Two steps and you can be inside. Then I'll try to disarm him.'

'No!' she whispered back. 'This is worse than before. He's beside himself and he doesn't know what he's doing. You'll be killed.'

'Stop your whispering and plotting because you won't get away,' Tim said, gaining in confidence. 'You're a murderer, Ryan Lanigan, and I'm here to see you pay.' And he raised the gun, pointing it at Ryan's heart.

'No, Tim, please listen to me.' Chrissie continued to stand in the line of fire. 'It was an accident. Everyone says so. Nobody wanted your father to die.'

'It's not fair. That man shot my father and walked free.'

'It was your father who brought that gun to the scene — not Ryan. And he lied to you too, saying it wasn't loaded.' Chrissie took a deep breath, trying to control her nerves. 'It was a terrible accident that shouldn't have happened. You don't want to make it worse by harming Ryan. Just drop the gun on the ground and step away.'

'Oh, you're so clever, making it sound so reasonable.' He put on a mocking falsetto. ' "Drop the gun on the ground and step away." You think I'll give up that easily? With revenge so close, I can almost taste it?' He raised the gun higher to point it at Ryan's head. His hand was shaking so much, Chrissie was afraid he'd fire it without really meaning to.

'This isn't you, Tim.' She felt bound to keep reasoning with him. 'You're not like your father.'

'Are you sure?' Tim giggled hysterically, betraying his nerves yet again. 'I might be exactly like him.'

Out of the corner of her eye, Chrissie could see the rest of the wedding party assembled in the hall looking out of the open front door, faces tense with horror at the scene being played out in front of them.

At that moment Tinka, sensing something was terribly wrong, dashed out of the house to start barking at Tim. For a small animal, she could make a very loud noise.

Momentarily distracted, Tim snarled, turning the gun towards the little dog bouncing around behind him. Chrissie clapped her hands to her mouth, certain Tinka was doomed, but it was Walter who surprised Tim, by coming up swiftly behind him, depriving him of the gun before he could fire it. Then, clearly used to firearms, he opened it and quickly removed the bullets.

'Hmm. Nasty little weapon,' he said, almost to himself. Then he looked up and grinned at the wedding party. 'Fine thing to have to do on our wedding day,' he said. 'But somebody better call the cops.'

Margie hurried to oblige.

Disarmed, all the courage and fight went out of Tim and he sank to the ground, hunched over his knees and weeping. There was no need to restrain him while they waited for the police to take him away.

'That poor kid,' Chrissie said later as they watched him being handcuffed and pushed none too gently into the back of a police car. The black sedan he arrived in had been reported as stolen. 'Never stood a chance in life, did he?'

'Well, nobody forced him to come here and ruin our wedding day,' Val said.

'He hasn't ruined it at all because we won't let him.' Walter was determined to raise everyone's spirits. 'I have a thirst above rubies! Let's get this party started and break out the champagne.'

## ON TRACK TO MURDER

### Heather Graves

Married at sixteen to a man over thirty years her senior, ten years on Larissa Barton begins to question the decision she made, especially when she discovers that Miles is cheating on her. All the same, she is shocked when Miles is the one to ask for a divorce. After leaving him, Larissa returns to her childhood home; she must rebuild her life with new friends. But Miles is jealous of his wife's new-found happiness, and he begins to use his power and influence to meddle in the lives of the people she loves . . .